"She likes being snuggled," Corinne whispered.

"I see that." Gabe was whispering, too. "I think you're both enjoying this."

"Immensely." She smiled. "The years are flying by with my kids. I miss this."

Her sweet regret painted another picture for him.

Corinne.

A baby.

A child to raise together.

The thought held an appealing mix of hope for the future. And then panic. His palms went damp, and he backed off from the image instantly.

"Do you want me to take her?" Part of him wanted her to say no while another part longed to protect.

She nodded and handed him Jessie. He leaned back, almost loving the feel of her on his chest, scared about how easy it would be to fall into a trap he couldn't afford—the trap of love.

He'd been there before and had nothing to show for it, but somehow holding Jessie made it feel almost possible…and that might be scarier yet.

Multipublished bestselling author **Ruth Logan Herne** loves God, her country, her family, dogs, chocolate and coffee! Married to a very patient man, she lives in an old farmhouse in upstate New York and thinks possums should leave the cat food alone and snakes should always live outside. There are no exceptions to either rule! Visit Ruth at ruthloganherne.com.

Books by Ruth Logan Herne

Love Inspired

Grace Haven

An Unexpected Groom
Her Unexpected Family
Their Surprise Daddy
The Lawman's Yuletide Baby

Kirkwood Lake

The Lawman's Second Chance
Falling for the Lawman
The Lawman's Holiday Wish
Loving the Lawman
Her Holiday Family

Men of Allegany County

Small-Town Hearts
Mended Hearts
Yuletide Hearts
His Mistletoe Family

Visit the Author Profile page at Harlequin.com for more titles.

The Lawman's Yuletide Baby

Ruth Logan Herne

Recycling programs
for this product may
not exist in your area.

LOVE INSPIRED BOOKS

ISBN-13: 978-0-373-89966-1

The Lawman's Yuletide Baby

Copyright © 2017 by Ruth M. Blodgett

Printed in U.S.A.

The Lord is close to the brokenhearted
and saves those who are crushed in spirit.
—*Psalms* 34:18

This book marks my twentieth book with Love Inspired, and I am blessed to be part of their outstanding group of authors. I am offering huge thanks, not only for this particular story, but for all those that have come before and are yet to come, to Melissa Endlich, my editor, guide and mentor, the person who took a chance on me in 2009 and launched a beautiful career with a phone message I still have on my voice mail—a voice mail I have never deleted because it marked a bend in the road I longed for all my life. So, to Melissa I say thank you. *Thank you so much.* And may God bless you.

Chapter One

This couldn't be happening.

Corinne Gallagher watched as the Realtor tacked a Sold sign on the year-round lakefront home less than a hundred feet from hers.

It wasn't the sign that made her heart take notice.

It was the man shaking the Realtor's hand.

New York State Trooper Gabe Cutler stood facing the real estate salesperson as if he'd just clinched the deal of a lifetime.

She swallowed hard as his gaze shifted from the Realtor to her.

Her heart ground to a painful stop.

So did her breath.

He stared at her, then her house, then her again.

She stood rooted to the ground, unable or maybe just unwilling to move.

Her twelve-year-old daughter had no such qualms. "Coach!" Theresa, known to the world as "Tee" Gallagher, streaked across the yard beneath a canopy of late October color. The blend of breeze and tinted leaves signaled another change of seasons.

Corinne was determined to ignore the passage of time.

It's what she did best.

Day by day, year by year, she looked forward, making sure her children were grounded, faithful, safe and kind. She purposely didn't look right or left. It was a job she did well because Corinne Gallagher did everything well.

"Coach, are you moving into the Penskis' house for real? Callan won't believe it!" Tee leaped at him, hugging the man who'd been coaching her brother for the last three years. Three very long years for Corinne to pretend she wasn't attracted to the decorated state trooper. Three years of watching him counsel and teach youngsters the rules of the game... and the rules of life. Three years of maintaining a distance because she would never willingly put herself in the position to bury another man in uniform.

He couldn't be moving in next door.

He lived nearly fifteen miles away, toward the south end of Canandaigua Lake, surrounded by vineyards. She'd Googled him on purpose during a weak moment.

Look at you. Stalking the baseball coach.

She hadn't stalked him. Not really. She'd just been curious. And lonely. And possibly wondering about the man behind the uniform, behind the stubborn set of his jaw as they met weekly to firm up the plans before the upcoming holiday-themed Christkindl festival.

And here he was, one arm around Tee, gazing her way.

This couldn't be happening.

And yet…it was.

"Coach, is that you?" Fourteen-year-old Callan poked his head out from the sliding glass door leading to the deck. "Are you kidding me? You're moving in next door? That's awesome!" The high school freshman loped across the yard, all arms and legs, a boy in the thick of adolescence. He pumped Gabe's hand, excited, then shoved his hands into his pockets as if unsure what to do with them.

Tee had no such qualms. She kept her arm linked through Gabe's as if she'd just acquired a new BFF. "Can you believe it, Mom?" She screeched the words as Corinne moved their way. "Coach is here! He's moving in! Right next door!"

Tee lived in a world full of exclamation

points. Nothing stagnated in Tee's world. Her roller-coaster personality kept life humming around her, a total contrast to her more sober older brother.

Callan took after Corinne, focused and cautious and steadfast.

Tee was total Gallagher, a feminine image of the father she'd never known. She was a spontaneous, fearless know-it-all, and there wasn't a day that went by when Corinne didn't thank God for these kids. They were a piece of Dave to keep close by her side, but that honor came with mega responsibility, a task she never took lightly.

"So." Gabe watched her approach.

Caramel-brown eyes, with hints of gold that brightened when he smiled. Medium brown hair, always cut short. Strong shoulders, a broad chest, made broader by his protective vest when he was in uniform.

But protective vests could only do so much. She'd found that out the hard way.

"We've just become neighbors." He didn't shift his gaze as she walked, and she didn't hurry her steps because she needed every single second to grab hold of the calm facade she'd need for this new bend in the road.

She nodded to the Realtor to gain a few extra seconds, then faced Gabe directly. "So it would seem. I had no idea you were looking for a house, Gabe."

He lifted one brow and paused, and when he did, her heart paused, too. "I didn't want to make a big deal out of it. I've always wanted to live in a quiet spot on the water. To throw my boat in now and again and drop a line. When this came on the market three weeks back, I knew it was perfect."

It wasn't perfect.

Having the strong, stoic trooper next door was the exact opposite of perfect.

Perfect was her safe, sound world, surrounded by Gallagher family and friends, a low-risk pool of normal.

Perfect was her administrative position at the hospital, where she'd graduated from the ups and downs of crisis pregnancy care to being a very capable paper pusher.

Ideal was having as much quiet control as she could get while not appearing to be one of those helicopter parents, hovering around everything their children did, thought or tried.

She'd tucked herself into this quiet corner of the lake, her grandparents' old house, determined to do things her way without appearing crazy neurotic.

Gabe Cutler's arrival just rocked a boat she'd kept calm for a long, long time.

* * *

Gabe Cutler had spent years purposely keeping himself on life's outer edges. He worked, he coached, he fished and he took good care of Tucker, his dog.

It was enough because he made it enough.

And now he'd managed to sign papers tucking him next door to Corinne Gallagher and her delightful kids, Callan and Tee.

How had this happened?

Corinne and the kids didn't live on the water. They lived in a simple split-level just off Route 20A. He'd dropped Callan off there a couple of times the year before.

And yet...

Here they were.

The kids looked delighted to see him, because they'd been buds for several years. He'd coached Callan, and laughed over Tee's antics.

Corinne looked surprised and maybe chagrined about the whole thing.

She helped with team stuff when she could. She organized fundraisers and structured team gatherings when they had out-of-town tournaments. She stayed friendly while keeping her distance, a neat trick she maneuvered well, which meant she was well practiced. Like him.

He smiled for a selfie with Callan, his star shortstop, then winced inside when Callan blasted the pic to the rest of the team with a wide, easy grin.

So much for keeping his private life private. A part of him wanted to sigh, because this was his fault for not checking the town's records before signing the purchase offer.

He wouldn't have chosen the house if he'd known Corinne and the kids lived next door. Gabe didn't just like his privacy. He craved it. He needed that downtime, where he could split wood or fish or do whatever he needed to do to get through the calendar year. And now—

Two bright-eyed kids, kids that he liked, grinned up at him as if this was a wonderful turn of events.

It wasn't anything of the kind.

"Is Tucker coming with you?"

The team loved his trusty mutt, a great dog. He'd rescued the tricolor collie mix from a shelter four years before, but it might have been the other way around. The goofy, loyal dog might have been the rescuer all along. "He is."

"Yes!" Tee fist-pumped the air. "Can I take him swimming? And for walks along the road? Because there is like no one living down here in the winter, Coach." She dramatized the words with perfect adolescent accentuation. "Well, a few people," she conceded. "But most of them go to Florida for the winter, so the road is crazy quiet now!"

And with all of those quiet, empty cottages dotting the shore, the only affordable house that had gone up for sale along the waterfront was right next to a busy, vibrant family. Was God laughing right now?

Although if this was some sort of master plan, Gabe failed to see the purpose. Or the humor, for that matter. "Tee Gallagher and a quiet road?" He hiked a brow that actually made Corinne smile. "Why does that seem hard to compute?"

"Even I can't make enough noise to liven up a whole road on my own," the girl told him. "But I do my best."

"That's for sure." Callan sent his text. He started to pocket his phone, but replies began flooding in, fast and furious. "My phone's blowing up, Coach." He laughed as he moved over to their honey-stained picnic table. "Gotta answer these."

"If I had a phone, I could share this news, too." Tee shifted her attention to Corinne.

"A conversation we've had way too often," Corinne told her. "You don't need a phone. When you're in high school, yes. I'll get you a phone and you can help pay for it. There's no need to do that now."

"Everyone in junior high has one. And I mean everyone."

A stat that didn't bode well in the school, Gabe knew. Some of those kids' phones were being used for things far beyond what a seventh grader should be considering, much less doing. He respected Corinne for taking a stand that clearly made her unpopular with her strong-willed daughter.

"Junior high kids have survived without phones for centuries. You'll be fine, Tee."

"Laura Ingalls didn't have a phone, so Tee Gallagher doesn't get one?" Tee hiked both brows, then rolled her eyes. "That's totally apples and oranges, Mom. Let's stay in the current century for comparison's sake." She shot Corinne a dimpled look, and Gabe couldn't hold back his smile.

The kid had sass.

She never gave up, she smiled a lot and she faced life fearlessly.

If Gracie had lived, he figured she'd be a lot like Tee Gallagher. But she didn't live. Neither did her mother. He had a host of regrets a mile long about that.

He'd messed up once.

He'd broken a good woman's heart and possibly her spirit, and the truth of that weighed heavily even nine years later.

He'd cost two lives that day. Three, if you counted his own by aftermath.

No, he couldn't afford to let this sweet family get under his skin. They treated him like he was a stand-up guy.

That's because they didn't know the truth. If they did, they'd think differently.

"Coach, I am just so crazy excited to have you here!" Tee hugged his arm again, and the shot of pain that jabbed his chest was quite real.

He realized that Gracie would have been Tee's age now. She would have had a mop of brown curls, and an unerring talent for winsome smiles, enough to grab his heart and hold it tight, all these years.

His chest constricted.

The real estate agent must have sensed the change in mood because she reached out a hand to Corinne. "You inherited this place from your parents, didn't you, Mrs. Gallagher?"

Corinne accepted the light handshake. "My grandmother, actually. Gram wanted to keep it in the family, and my late husband loved the water. He said you could learn more about a woman by watching the lake change than any self-help book on the market."

The Realtor laughed. "My husband would

agree. Well, if you ever think about selling, give me a call." She handed Corinne a business card. "I know you haven't been back on the water for long, but we never have enough lakefront property to fill the demand. No pressure, of course."

Corinne stared at the card, and Gabe felt like a complete jerk. Was she really that bothered because he moved in next door? Or because he'd disagreed with her stance on the Christmas festival committee the week before? Would she really stay upset about that?

He didn't know her well enough to know, but he hoped not.

"Coach, when are you moving in?" Callan's excitement lightened the moment. "I can help if it's on the weekend."

"I closed the deal this morning, and I'm working this weekend, so next weekend is move-in time."

"Mom." Callan swung around. "I bet me and some of the guys—"

"And me!" Tee cut in.

Callan frowned at her, then continued, "I bet we could help Coach get everything moved. What do you think?"

The kid meant well, but he'd just corralled his mother, so Gabe stepped in. "Listen, Corinne, if you're working that weekend, it's no problem." He was offering her an out if she wanted to take it. "I know your schedule can get complicated."

"Not anymore." Tee caroled the words. "Mom isn't doing regular nursing anymore. She's got an office and she's one of the people who make sure everything gets done right."

"You've moved up?" She nodded, but looked more resigned than happy, as if moving up the ladder of success wasn't all it was cracked up to be. "That's a big change."

"Takes some getting used to," she told him, then directed her attention to Callan. "Cal, I think it would be great for you guys to help Coach move in. If he wants the help, that is."

What could he say and not sound like a total curmudgeon? "I'd love it."

"And then we can do hot dogs and stuff at our house if the weather stays nice," Tee exclaimed. "Right, Mom? You're here on the weekends now, and if the guys haul all Coach's stuff, we can make food for them, just like Grandma does whenever we do things. She always makes it so special to help."

"Your grandma has a way of putting a shine on life like no other woman I've ever known. Except possibly your Aunt Kimberly," Corinne conceded. "Tee, that sounds like a great idea. If it's all right with Coach."

"What kind of guy would refuse an offer of help and food?" He gave Tee a half hug, then dropped his arm. "Sounds like a plan. And now." He turned back to the Realtor. "I've got to head home and get ready for work. I'm on the late shift today."

"Like at night?" Tee asked.

He nodded. "We switch things up. I don't do nights as much as I used to, but I told them I'd help out as needed from now through December." He didn't mention that he grabbed whatever hours he could late in the year. Working didn't just keep him busy during the deluge of holiday forums embraced by their sweet, small town. It kept him sane. "We've got a couple of guys who needed day shifts. And one who just had a baby, so he's out for a couple of weeks. I think they were in your unit, actually." He lifted his eyes to Corinne. "Jason and Shelly Montgomery. Shelly had some problems, and was in the hospital for the last four weeks, then the baby was in the NICU for a few weeks. But now everyone is home, no one is sleeping and life is good."

"I heard they were a very nice couple. I didn't know Jason was a trooper."

That surprised him, because the baseball parents seemed to open up to Corinne, and then he put two and two together. "Of course, the new job. Off the floor. So you wouldn't get to know people the same way. Well." He stepped back. "Gotta go. I'll see you guys at tomorrow night's game."

"Last game of fall ball," said Tee. "And then we blast right into the holidays. This will be our first Christmas on the water! Maybe we can decorate the dock and everything, like Grandpa used to do!"

Callan reached out and pumped Gabe's hand. "This is great, Coach! Really great! I can't believe it!"

It wasn't great. It was the opposite of great because Gabe Cutler didn't do holidays. He didn't do family gatherings or twinkle lights, and if he could disengage himself from endless loops of sappy carols, he'd do it in a heartbeat. Holidays forced him to think about what he'd lost.

And now he'd be next door to twinkle lights–loving Tee and her intrinsic optimism.

Corinne was watching him. Her brows shifted together in concern. Because he'd slipped and let his dark side show?

Maybe.

But then she hid that emotion and began backpedaling to her place. "Kids, let's go so Coach can get to work. We've got homework and laundry waiting for us."

"And then can we take the boat out?" Tee gazed at the water with longing. "You said we could this weekend. You promised."

Corinne tapped her watch. "All depends on time, kid. Let's roll."

Callan strode back toward the house.

Tee slumped her shoulders. "I don't know why we live on a lake when we can't ever do anything on the lake."

"Yeah, yeah, yeah." Corinne reached to put an arm around Tee's shoulders.

The girl shrugged her off, chin down.

Corinne looked at Tee, then him, then lifted her hands. "Welcome to the neighborhood, Gabe, where moods change faster than the weather, and that's mighty fast around here."

She was right. Weather on the water could be unpredictable. That's one of the things he loved about it.

Would Gracie have loved the water like he did?

He'd never know. He'd never know her favorite color, her favorite song, her favorite dolls because she was gone too soon.

He wanted to remind Corinne how precious life was. He wanted to encourage her to leave the stupid laundry and fire up that outboard. The changing seasons meant fewer trips on the water.

He kept quiet on purpose.

She knew the pros and cons, just like he did. She'd also loved and lost, and didn't need his advice. And after working together on the intertown baseball league, and then the festival committee, he was pretty sure she wouldn't take his advice, anyway.

She wasn't cool or judgmental or obnoxious, but she kept her guard in place.

Uptight people tended to annoy him because he'd grown up surrounded by them. His mother's family lived their lives tightly wound about everything from religion to politics to food choices.

And yet, with all they had, all the blessings abounding, they were never satisfied. Never content. His mother wasn't like that. Neither was Gabe.

He'd lost his contentment through his own fault. But it bothered him when folks didn't understand the blessings of a child. Any child. And how, if he had it to do all over again, he'd make whatever sacrifice needed to keep a kid safe and happy and content.

So you'd give Tee a phone? Even though you know better?

He wouldn't, he realized, as Tee stomped into her house. He'd do exactly what Corinne was doing, but he'd hate every single stinkin' minute of it.

But it would never be an issue because he'd had his chance once and blew it. And that was that.

And here he was, next door to a woman who kept a cool distance in what she did. Not exactly an ice queen, but not all that warm, either.

The sale was complete.

The deed had changed hands. He'd have to make the best of it. So would she.

Corinne resisted change. She wasn't a fighter, but she quietly blocked it in her own way.

Did she know how blessed she was to have those two kids? He couldn't look at Tee and not remember Gracie. And a fine kid like Callan, hardworking and devoted to playing ball. A young man, ready to explore so much of the world around him.

Not your business.

He knew that. And it wouldn't become his business, no matter how pretty those blue eyes were when she looked his way.

He'd made a promise when he laid his baby girl into the ground, a pledge he intended to keep. He'd been given the gold ring once and lost it by his lack of attention.

He'd laid flowers on her grave and promised

God he'd never take that chance again, and he meant every word, but when Corinne Gallagher waved from her back deck, his fickle heart tried to pry itself open.

He slammed it shut.

He'd had it all once and ruined it. He had absolutely no right to wish for more than what he had now. A great job keeping people safe, a small boat and a house on the water.

A house that seemed pretty empty compared with the busy family living next door.

Chapter Two

Gabe had just finished packing dozens of boxes when his landline phone rang the following Saturday. He almost tripped getting through the confusing maze, but when he saw his mother's number in the display, he grabbed the call quickly. "Hey, Mom. What's up?"

"Gabe. Do you have a minute?"

Worry wrenched her voice. He was pretty sure she was crying, and he was nearly four hours away with a moving crew on the way, but if she needed him, he'd hop in the car and head toward Albany because Linda Cutler had gone the distance for him too many times to count. And with his mother's crazy, mixed-up, dysfunctional family, Gabe knew he'd been blessed to be on the normal end of the spectrum. "Of course I do. Take your time. I'm right here."

"I know. I just..." She breathed out a sigh. "Aunt Maureen just got off the phone with me, screaming about life's injustices, and how unfair things are. She's blaming the police and the world for everything that went wrong with Adrianna. I tried to calm her down, but it didn't work. She hung up on me, but not before she called me unkind names."

"I'm sure she's hurting, but that's no reason to take it out on you. I'm sorry, Mom. You know Aunt Maureen. It's always someone else's fault." His narrow-minded aunt had recently buried the daughter she'd disowned years before. Adrianna had gotten herself into a mess of trouble as a teen, then again as a young adult. She'd done time, and her parents made sure that everyone knew they wanted nothing to do with their wayward child.

She'd died in a convenience store robbery gone bad, a tragic end to a life filled with flawed choices.

"My sister is mean, Gabe. Just plain mean, and it's got nothing to do with her faith or her church, it's her. No wonder that poor girl went rogue. And now look what it's all come to."

She was right. His mom's younger sister had a sharp tongue and always held a grudge. She and his uncle had little regard for Christ's instruction on forgiveness. "Aunt Maureen is probably second-guessing her actions, Mom— maybe wishing she hadn't thrown Adrianna out of the house, or been so strict with her."

"Or she's blaming everyone but herself for her family problems."

That sounded more like it. "Do you want me to come down there? I can. I've got the next two days off." He didn't mention that he was supposed to be moving because she'd refuse his help if she thought she was inconveniencing him.

She'd blessed him from the day he was born, or at least as far back as he could remember. She'd been a single mom at a time when being a single mother wasn't overtly accepted, but she'd been great. And still was.

And through it all, her sister Maureen had held Linda's mistakes up like a banner, making sure everyone knew that Linda lived a life of bad choices.

But in the end, Gabe had turned out just fine and Maureen's two daughters had brought nothing but trouble on themselves. That had always infuriated his fire-and-brimstone aunt. "Why did you take her call?"

"Because she just lost her daughter."

Gabe would have done the same. "Do you want to come up here for a visit?"

"No, I just needed to vent. Maureen is just…"

She paused, then drew a deep breath. "Well, you know. She needs to lay this at someone else's door, and that finger of blame will never fall back on her. Maybe if she'd shown those girls a little kindness, a little understanding—" She paused again. "No use rehashing all of that. And you're right, if she calls again, I'll let it go to voice mail. I'm working overtime this weekend, so that will gain me some distance."

His mother worked at a manufacturing facility outside Albany. "You sure you're okay?"

"Yes, I just needed someone to talk to. It's been a rough couple of months down here, and losing Adrianna like that has stirred some old pots."

"Aunt Maureen and Uncle Blake had choices, Mom. So did Adrianna."

"I know. And I knew I could only do so much when their mother was dead set against anyone helping those girls out, but it weighs on me, Gabe, knowing Adrianna longed for help and thought no one would provide it."

Guilt.

It was an emotion he knew well. Too well. "We pray, Mom. And we keep our eyes open for other ways to help people. Like you taught me all along." The noise of pickup trucks pulling into the driveway made him turn. "You sure you don't want me to head down there? I can be there by lunchtime."

"I'm sure. Just glad you don't mind talking with your mom now and again."

"Mind?" He laughed because throughout his times of trouble, Linda Cutler had been the calm voice of faith, hope and reason. "I love it, Mom. And I love you."

He pictured her smile in the softer note in her voice. "I love you, too. Bye, honey."

He hung up, knowing she'd be okay, but it wasn't easy to dodge angry family members, especially when proximity allowed them access.

That was another reason he'd moved four hours northwest when everything fell apart. Distance from his mother's family wasn't a choice, it had been a lifesaving measure.

The first two trucks rolled to a stop, and half a dozen boys and men aimed for his door. He swung it wide in welcome.

He might not have family here, but between the troopers and the baseball team, his needs were covered.

By ten o'clock they were on their way to 2312 Lakeshore Drive with the first wave of belongings.

He thought it would take all day to move things.

He was wrong.

A single guy who worked long hours and coached three seasons of baseball didn't accumulate a lot of stuff.

They pulled the trucks into the lakefront driveway one at a time. Tee spotted them and raced across the narrow yards, hurdling the short privet hedge on the property line. "Can I help?"

He spotted Corinne's bemused expression next door. Hands up, she gestured to the tables and chairs she'd been setting out and then her daughter. "You help here," he told her. "I'll go help your mother move the tables."

"Oops." Looking a little guilty, Tee spun and waved. "Sorry, Mom!"

"I'll bet she is," Corinne noted as Gabe drew closer. "She'd much rather help the team than be stuck helping her mother."

"Pretty normal, I expect. But I can help her mother," Gabe added as he lifted one of the tables. "Tell me where you want them and I'll get them in order for you."

"You've got a whole house to arrange," she scolded. "I can handle this."

Gabe moved the first table closer to the lake as he replied, "I've got bedroom stuff, kitchen stuff and living room stuff, which means half the rooms of the house will sit empty. I bet they can figure it out, Corinne. And my buddy

Mack is over there with his wife, and when Susie MacIntosh takes charge, we all smile and nod and follow orders."

"My kind of gal." Corinne started setting up folding chairs. "Should we start the fire now, if you guys don't have to make too many more trips back to your old place?"

"One more trip should do it, so that's probably a good idea." He settled the next table close to the first. "And if I'm setting these in the wrong spots, tell me. Don't wait until I'm gone, then change them."

"Well, it's a simple afternoon barbecue, so I'm pretty sure anywhere is good."

Her tone was easy, but it didn't take a real smart guy to sense something amiss. "Listen, Corinne. I didn't get a chance to talk to you after the committee meeting the other night." He was working as the safety liaison for the upcoming Christkindl festival, a huge annual event that netted tens of thousands of dollars for the Police Benevolence Fund. The fund helped widows and children of fallen officers. As a widow, Corinne had headed the committee for half a dozen years, but the current committee had voted in some major changes she didn't like. Changes he approved, which might make him persona non grata with his new neighbor.

"Because you were mobbed by triumphant town retailers and I had to get home to the kids."

That was true, but law enforcement was schooled in undercurrents, and the one on this deck rivaled an East Coast riptide. "I don't want you to think we were trying to undercut your position."

A momentary pause of her hands was her only outward reaction, which meant she was hiding her feelings, a move he recognized because he'd hidden his share. Watching her, he realized she was just as good as he was at disguising his true emotions. Maybe better. "When you, Lizzie and Maura took places on the committee, it meant we all needed to work together," she replied in a soft, even voice. "Although neither Kate nor I was invited to the impromptu meeting you guys had on Tuesday."

It hadn't been a meeting at all. He'd run into two other committee members at the Bayou Barbecue, and the two women had hijacked his quiet supper with committee talk.

"It wasn't a meeting. I was having supper at Josie's place. Lizzie and Maura came in and sat down, so we compared notes. Then I got a call on the south end of the lake, and Josie bagged my food for later. That's all it was, pure coincidence."

"You don't owe me explanations, Gabe."

He didn't...but he did. Corinne had invested years in this festival because she'd buried a first responder, and he didn't take that lightly. Nor should anyone else. "I do, because Lizzie made it sound like we held a prearranged meeting. It wasn't anything of the kind."

"And yet there's no reason it couldn't be, is there, Gabe?" She paused again, watching him from the far side of the deck, holding a floral porch pillow in her hands. She looked... cautiously beautiful, if there was such a thing, and there must be, because he was seeing it, right now.

No reason...

"Of course there's a reason. To go behind your back and usurp the time and effort you've put into this whole thing would be ludicrous. I can't imagine someone doing that, and if they did, they'd have to answer to me. That's not how things are done, Corinne. Not in police brotherhoods, anyway."

She watched him, still clutching the pillow, and when he was done with his little spiel, she still watched.

And then she smiled, ever so slightly, as she set the pillow down.

Her smile intrigued him.

He wasn't sure why, because she did absolutely nothing to try to intrigue him. In fact, she went out of her way to be carefully level and polite, like the model nurses you saw on TV.

As she looked down, her lips quirked up, as if he'd pleased her.

He wasn't looking to please anyone. He'd won the race once. He'd had it all until he lost it, way too quick and far too easy.

Yes, he was older. Smarter. But he was just as guilty now as he'd been when Gracie climbed into his SUV all those years ago. A stupid football party, parents, kids, pizza and beer...

He swallowed hard. "I just didn't want you thinking we were plotting behind your back. Or Kate's back." Corinne's mother-in-law had built a highly regarded event business in Grace Haven. She'd shared her expertise by helping with the festival for years.

"Kate's a smart woman. She saw the way things were trending from the beginning, and that's why she volunteered to work with Lizzie and Maura."

"To keep an eye on them?"

"That sounds far too sinister, even for a small town." She crossed the decking and moved more chairs into place. "More like she wants to keep her finger on the pulse of the area. When you run an event center, it's important to be on the inside informational loop. And I'm sure she wanted to keep me updated so I wouldn't get clotheslined by whatever changes came about. Kate knows I'm busy, and she takes an understandable special interest in the benevolence fund."

Of course she did. She'd buried a son, and her husband had been chief of police for over twenty years. The Gallaghers appreciated law enforcement like few families could. They'd lived it for over two generations. "She's protective of you."

"Sure she is." She drew up more chairs. "They love me, and they love these kids. That's pretty much how the family rolls. And they know being a single mom isn't easy. But we're doing okay."

After being raised in a single-parent house, he knew the truth of it, and it was never an easy gig to be top provider, rule maker and beloved parent to kids. "I'd say you're doing great, Corinne."

"Well. Thank you." She took the compliment lightly. Maybe too lightly. "It's too early to start the grill, but if you call me from the truck, I'll have it heated up when you guys get back."

"Sounds good." He touched a long-nosed

lighter to the kindling in the fire pit, waiting for the first flickers of success. "If you ever need anything…" He waited until she looked up, and when she did, there it was again. A tiny spark of connection when his eyes met hers. "Call me, okay? I'm right over there, and I'm happy to help."

"That's a really nice offer." Sincerity deepened her tone, while her expression stayed matter-of-fact. "The Penskis were gone a lot, so I'd only seen them twice since we moved in last year. And when the weather turns, it's kind of desolate down here. Like Tee said, most folks use these as summer homes, so there aren't too many neighbors during the winter. It will be nice to have you nearby."

He puffed on the kindling until a curl of smoke burst into tiny licks of flame. "I saw that little park at the end of the road by the turnoff. It's got a small baseball field."

"A relic from times past, when neighborhoods got together to play ball. That's Welch Grove Park."

"It's quiet and I can practice ball with the kids there whenever they're available."

"I played ball on that field when I was a girl." She tapped the grill as if tapping home plate and took a batter's stance.

"You lived here?"

"Off and on, with my grandparents."

She didn't elaborate and it wasn't his business to delve, but why hadn't she been with her parents?

Not his business, so he kept to baseball. "They had softball there?"

"Hardball."

She'd surprised him again. "You played hardball?"

"Seven years. When I got to high school girls could only play softball, and that's a whole other game." She moved a chair that didn't need moving and shrugged. "I moved on to other things. That's why I loved seeing Amy make the team when Drew Slade came back to town. A girl with that kind of talent shouldn't be relegated to a minimal role in anything."

"If you're good enough, you play." It made sense to him, regardless of gender.

"That's something you and I can agree on." She didn't mention the festival controversy per se, but he understood the meaning behind the words.

"Gabe." Mack called his name from across the yards. "We need to know how you want some of the things set up."

"Coming." He tipped his ball cap slightly. "One more load to get, and that should do it on our end. I'll be happy to man the grill when we get back."

"I am delighted to accept the offer."

"Good."

He jogged back to his place.

He'd hurried over there to clear the air over Thursday's meeting. She'd lost an important battle, one that meant she'd be facing angry vendors at the upcoming holiday festival. The out-of-town vendors had paid a significant fee to contract their space on the grounds of the historic Gallagher farm at the edge of town. They weren't expecting to have local buses transporting their shoppers downtown every fifteen minutes. There would be backlash, mostly directed at Corinne because she headed the committee. It wasn't her fault, and he felt bad about that. He'd sided with the local businesses from a practical angle. Putting Corinne in the crosshairs hadn't been the intention, but it was a probable outcome.

Would she hold a grudge?

He hoped not, but her guarded nature didn't make her an easy read.

"Coach, I can't wait for you to see how many fish there are in the lake! Grandpa showed me so many hot spots, it's amazing! Do you like perch and bass?" Tee grabbed his hand in an excited grip as he crossed the yard.

He loved both. He nodded as the old weight redescended.

"Then maybe we can go fishing sometime together," Tee exclaimed. "I can ask Mom, I bet she won't mind, and I won't be noisy. I know not to be noisy on the boat, because Grandpa threatened to toss me overboard if I scared the fish. And I love eating fish, so why would I scare them?"

She talked at light speed, like Gracie had.

Her hands danced in the air, alive with excitement.

Her eyes so blue.

Gracie's had been a lighter shade of blue, tinged green, but with that same kind of sparkle and joy.

Gone.

His heart choked.

So did his voice, because he couldn't form a word around the massive lump clogging his throat.

He'd thought it would get better in time, and it had, but when he was around Tee Gallagher and her crew of funny, adolescent girlfriends, all he could think of was how sweetly Gracie would have fit into their crowd. Laughing, dancing, climbing…

"Come with me." Susie MacIntosh thrust

her arm through his and propelled him into the house. "Focus on the simple and the mundane."

Susie had known him all those years ago, years before they both moved upstate to Grace Haven.

"You've got to forgive yourself, Gabe. God doesn't want you to spend your life beating yourself up. He wants you whole and happy again."

Susie's opinion was similar to the reverend's talk last Sunday.

And maybe it would have worked out that way, if Elise had been okay. But she wasn't all right, ever again. Then she was gone, too.

"We make choices, Gabe. All of us. You, me, Mack. Elise."

He couldn't listen to this, because there was no way he could lay any of this on Elise. He'd left the door of the SUV slightly open. He must have. He was the last person in it. He'd pulled into his buddy's driveway and parked. Then he'd gotten Gracie out of her car seat and walked into the broad backyard of Jim Clayton, another state trooper.

He was the designated driver, so he grabbed some cold iced tea and talked NFL prospects, waiting for the four o'clock kickoff in Jim's man cave–style barn toward the back of the property.

And then came the scream.

Nine years later, he still heard the scream.

Elise's voice, screaming his name, screaming for help, and Gracie Lynn, their beautiful little girl, lying so still in the grueling heat of the SUV.

Her death was ruled accidental, but he knew better. He was her father. She was his responsibility, and he'd failed her over football stats and arguments about team superiority. All while his baby girl lay perishing in the unyielding temperatures of an SUV parked beneath a brilliant September sun.

No, there were no second chances for stupid fathers.

God was big enough to forgive because he was God.

But Gabe was a mere man, and there was no way on this earth he could forgive himself. And that was that.

Chapter Three

The group of young movers crossed from Gabe's yard into hers when the final load had been brought and distributed, but Corinne's heart went into overdrive as the tall, square-shouldered policeman followed in their wake. Gabe Cutler, chatting with "Mack" MacIntosh, another local trooper.

"Mom, we're going to check out the cove, okay?" Callan and five of his teammates got to her first.

"No swimming," she reminded them. "It's too cold for that."

"No swimming. But we might throw Tee into the water, just because she's a pest."

Tee pretended innocence, but Corinne knew the truth. Tee was a hoot, but she could be a pain in the neck to her big brother, and no way did she want the twelve-year-old hanging out with fourteen-and fifteen-year-old boys. "I'm keeping Tee here to help me. You guys did all the heavy lifting. We're doing food."

"Mom." Tee folded her arms and scowled. "Girls don't have to stay home and cook while the brave hunter goes in search of food anymore. We can actually *do* things, just like they can. It's called the new millennium." She hooked her thumb toward the teenage ballplayers, heading for the cove up the beach. "I could have helped move things. And I should be able to go to the cove. I'm twelve."

"I know how old you are. I was present at your birth, remember?"

But Tee saw nothing amusing in her reply. "We've got food ready, and everything's done. Why can't I go?"

What could she say? That she wasn't sure the boys' conversations would be okay for Tee's ears? And that Callan deserved some time away from his nosy little sister?

The boys were good kids, but they were hormone-struck teens, and she wasn't ready to have to deal with Tee and crushes and heartbreaks. Why had the idea of kids spaced so close together appealed to her a dozen years ago?

Oh, that's right.

Because she didn't know any better.

Tee huffed into the house as Gabe, Susie and Mack climbed the short steps on one side while the boys raced across the short stretch of open beach. "They did a great job today."

"I'm so glad." She opened the grill, judged it ready and pointed out the grilling tools hanging from a head-high two-by-four. "Tools of the trade. And the meat is in the cooler. Where's Tucker?"

"I put him in the house. He'll need to get a feel for his boundaries, so for now he's napping on the floor. Or staring at us through the sliding glass doors, which seems to be more accurate at the moment."

They all turned. The black, brown and white dog peered at them through the glass, tongue lolling, hoping they'd notice.

"That's a tough face to ignore," noted Mack.

"And he knows it. But better safe than sorry." He moved toward the cooler. "I'll save him a hot dog. Tucker forgives anything if there's a hot dog involved."

"I wonder if there's a similar system that works on kids," Corinne mused. "It's definitely cheaper than a cell phone, which is our current argument of the day."

"Tee doesn't let things go, does she?"

"No. And I hate being the bad guy 24/7, but that's kind of how things shake down."

Understanding marked his gaze. "My mom said that, too. She raised me on her own, and she always said the hardest part was being the tough one, all the time. No respite. But it worked out in the end."

"That's my hope and prayer, right there. That they grow up to have full and happy lives. Like you did."

His face drew down slightly as he began laying the meat on the hot grill surface. She started to chat with Susie as the hamburgers, hot dogs and Italian sausage sent meat-scented smoke their way.

Corinne breathed deeply, loving the scents of a cookout on the lake. Susie turned a pale shade of gray-green and looked dreadful.

Pregnant.

Corinne had dealt with morning sickness both personally and on a professional level. She took Susie's hand and led her toward the house. "I'm going to show Susie around inside. You guys okay?"

"Just fine."

"Yup." Mack lifted a cold bottle of iced tea their way. "See you in a few."

She got Susie inside to the bathroom just in time, then gave her a cool, damp washcloth to lay across her forehead. "Sit down and breathe easy, and it will pass."

"I'm so embarrassed." Susie's mouth scrunched up below the wet cloth. "Corinne, you don't even know me."

"No time like the present." Corinne laughed. "But I've seen this particular malady often enough because I'm a nurse in the crisis pregnancy unit. How far along are you?"

"Eighteen weeks. But we've kept it pretty quiet because pregnancy hasn't gone well with us."

"Susie, I'm sorry."

Susie shrugged beneath the cool cloth, but her chin quivered. "I'm with a new doctor and she's determined. And I've never been sick like this before."

"A well-set pregnancy makes its presence known."

"Is that true?" Susie sat up and whisked the damp cloth from her forehead. "Because the doctor said that, too."

"It is in my experience. And I'm putting you on my prayer list right now because this would be so exciting." She reached over and pressed Susie's hand lightly. "A new baby coming to visit the lake next spring." A baby...so sweet, so special, such an amazing blessing. And so very difficult for some. She saw that on her hospital unit. She'd dealt with the mercurial highs and lows of crisis pregnancy.

She'd wanted a house full of kids. She'd wanted to chase babies and toddlers and push strollers long after Tee was running and climbing and shrugging off any offers of help. Her dream had been thwarted by a felon's bullet, but she had two beautiful children, and that was something to be grateful for.

She spotted movement on the deck. "Susie, pretend you're looking at something."

"Which I am, of course." Susie picked up a book from the table as Mack came to the sliding screen door separating them from the broad wooden deck.

"How we doing in there?"

"We've finished the grand tour and Susie's checking out a book I recommended."

"Great." He smiled through the screen at his wife. "Gabe says we've got about five minutes until everything's done."

"I'll bring out the rest of the stuff. Susie, feel free to borrow that and tell me what you think."

"Thank you, Corinne."

"Tee?" Corinne called upstairs from the first floor. "Can you help me with food?" Long seconds of silence ensued before she heard Tee's footsteps on the floor above.

Shouts from up the beach indicated the boys' return. Corinne carried a hot potato salad out to the deck. Tee followed with a cold pasta salad, and dragged her feet every inch of the way, right up until the boys made it to the deck.

Then everything changed.

Tee raised her chin.

Her eyes sparkled.

Shoulders back, she was the epitome of charm once the deck was filled with five young baseball players.

Corinne wanted to smack a hand to her head, because if Tee was crushing on one of Callan's friends, the result could be gut-wrenching for brother and sister.

Callan loved Tee. He'd given her that name as a toddler. She was his "Tee-Tee," and the name stuck.

But they were stepping into uncharted waters now.

And while Corinne didn't have to do too many weekend shifts anymore, the idea of teens with too much time on their hands was worrisome. Time alone and internet access, texting, unlimited phone use...

She wanted normal for these two, but how could she strike that balance, keep them safe and allow them to grow in current times?

"She's got a thing for Brandon."

Gabe's soft voice made her turn. "You think?" Brandon was the team's center fielder.

"Oh, yeah. She's being subtle around him and a little too loud with the other boys, as if trying to gain his attention. And he's oblivious."

Corinne glanced behind her and agreed. "Can I lock her away? At least until sophomore year of college?"

He laughed softly as he removed meat from the grill. "I think that's an excellent idea. And this road is out of the way enough that the boys won't be visiting down here, unless they're coming to see Callan."

"Which they do on a regular basis."

He exaggerated a wince. "That means team dynamics are about to change. We'll go from total dedication to the game to split attention because of *G-I-R-L-S*. There goes our guaranteed spot in the state playoffs."

She couldn't help it. She laughed. "We're not that bad, are we?"

"At that age?" He raised the tongs and indicated the boys and one lovestruck tween. "No contest."

He was right. There was nothing like the bittersweet moments of young romance to mess with a kid's head.

She dreaded it, not because she didn't want the kids to grow up. That was normal. But the older they got, the less she could fix for them, and affairs of the heart were not easily mended.

She sighed because she knew the truth in that. Broken romances were mended only by time, faith and experience. "No one asked my opinion on this particular timeline, but if asked, I'd have put it off another year. Or two."

"And yet, no one offers options," Mack said as he came up alongside them. "We deal with what comes our way, the good and the bad."

Gabe's jaw tightened. He stared down as he flipped the meat, then piled it all onto her large platter. "I'll put the meat on the ledge."

He didn't look at Mack. He didn't look at her. He crossed the open patio overlooking the water, set the tray down and walked to the water's edge.

Mack scrubbed a hand to his jaw, watching Gabe. Then he sighed, turned and called out to the guys. "Food's ready!"

"Great!"

"Awesome!"

"Thanks for doing this, Mrs. G.!"

The grown-ups waited while the boys filled their plates, and when they all gravitated toward the water—and their beloved coach—the adults had a quiet patio to themselves.

Gabe stayed by the water, talking with the boys. Should she go get him? Remind him that the food was getting cold? He'd been fine, working, cooking, talking, and then…not fine.

He started their way a few minutes later.

He didn't look at her. Didn't look at anyone, not really. If alone in a crowd had a face, it was Gabe Cutler's expression, right now.

"The burgers came out perfect, Gabe. Thank you for cooking them."

"Happy to help."

But he didn't look happy at all. He kept his gaze averted and his shoulders square as if a wall had sprung up between him and the rest of the world.

Just as well.

Once the busyness of his move settled down, she'd keep a comfortable distance because she wasn't a moonstruck adolescent.

She was a grown woman who'd already buried one lawman. Nothing in this world would make her take a chance on facing that a second time.

Chapter Four

Gabe faced a new normal through his spacious lakefront picture window later that afternoon. His shaded yard tapered down to a strip of sandy beach. The dock stood to the right of the property line. Corinne's was on the left of her line, offering a wide expanse of sweet, shallow water.

Tucker would love living here.

He'd given his trusty friend a tour of the yard on a leash, reminding him of boundaries. Tucker learned quickly, but Gabe wanted to make sure he understood the commands of a new place. Chasing a rabbit up the hill to the much-busier four-lane road could be deadly, so a little time spent now was well worth it until the dog felt acclimated.

Him or you?

The mental question had Gabe scratching the back of his head.

Corinne was right. The lake was quiet in the fall. Maybe too quiet. He liked quiet in theory, but there was a soothing monotony in the noise and traffic and activity of a busy country road.

There was no busy on Lakeshore Drive in November. That meant he better do something to create his own distractions. A dozen stuffed packing boxes on the second floor should do it.

He went upstairs. He and Mack and one of the team dads had set up the furniture. Susie had put sheets and blankets on the bed, and she'd freshened the pillowcases. She'd probably cringed while doing it, because Gabe didn't swap them out as often as he should, but she faced his grimy cases like a true friend.

That made him smile as he pulled another box open and began putting things in drawers.

A noise made him pause.

He looked outside, then down the hall and saw nothing.

Heard nothing.

He moved back to the room and resumed his task, one thing after another.

It came again. A noise. A small noise, like a tiny animal's cry.

He had the front windows open to the fresh fall air. He peered out. A bird, maybe?

But then Tucker barked down below. He barked again as Gabe came across the open hallway above, then the big dog paced back and forth by the door. "Have you got to go out again, fella?"

Tucker panted by the street-side door, paced, then panted again.

The noise came again, closer now.

Tucker bounded up, laying two big front paws against the hardwood door, and he barked, twice.

"Down."

The dog came down.

Gabe gave him a hand command to sit and be quiet. Tucker obeyed quickly but kept his canine attention locked on the door.

Gabe peeked outside from the side window, one hand on the weapon he carried in his back waistband.

Was someone casing the place? Skulking around?

Woven vines along the lattice blocked his view of the small covered porch. He kept his hand on the gun and quietly opened the door.

His heart stopped. And then he dropped his hands, leaving the weapon right where it was.

A baby.

Sound asleep. In a car seat. On his front step.

He stared for too many seconds, then dropped down as if someone had drawn a bead on him.

The baby sighed, thought to stick a hand into a tiny mouth, then thought better of it and dozed back off, utterly content.

His heart stopped.

A diaper bag lay next to the baby. And the baby's wrappings appeared clean and fresh, although the car seat carrier looked worn.

Snugged in pink...

A girl, then? Most likely.

He reached out a tentative hand, then realized he was being foolish. She wasn't going to explode if he touched her and she couldn't stay outside on the stoop. He lifted the carrier and brought her inside.

She frowned, wriggled, then dozed right back off.

A baby.

He scratched his head and never thought twice about what he did next. He crossed the room, swung open his door and hollered for Corinne. She popped out of her sliding glass door with reading glasses perched on her head and waved. "What's up? Do you need something?"

"Can you come over here? Now?"

"Of course." She slipped into a pair of canvas shoes sitting on the deck and crossed the yards. "What's wrong?"

He pointed.

She followed the direction of his hand. Her mouth dropped open in a perfect circle. "It's a baby."

"Yup."

"Whose?"

He shook his head. "I have no idea."

"What?" Disbelief formed a W between her eyes. "That's impossible."

"It's quite possible, actually. I came down from upstairs and there she was, on the front porch stoop, sound asleep."

"No note?"

He crossed to the bag and rummaged around. "I didn't look. I was too surprised by the baby."

"A little girl." Corinne whispered the words and sounded absolutely joyful as she did. "Oh, Gabe, she is beautiful."

"Except no one in their right mind abandons a beautiful baby."

"A mother needing sanctuary for her child, maybe? You are a cop and you work in a sanctuary building."

"Except this is my home. Not the troop house." He pulled a zippered pocket of the bag open and found a thick envelope inside.

It wasn't sealed and he yanked out a sheaf of papers quickly. The first sheet was a letter, to him, and it was signed by his late cousin, Adrianna.

Gabe,
If you're reading this, it's because I'm gone. My friend Nita and I had this all worked out, and I was going to bring Jess to you, but I'm not sure what will happen now. These guys, the guys I'm working with, well…they don't care. Not about themselves, not about their women, and they sure don't care about innocent babies.

I stayed sober a long time, Gabe, but I'm not straight now and I can't live with myself if something happens to her because I'm stupid and selfish. I tried to give her up to strangers, but I couldn't do it. I just couldn't.

You're the best person I know. My parents disowned me and they want nothing to do with Jessie. They called her a child of sin. My sister has her hands full. Her husband left when he lost his job, and that's a mess.

I have no one else, Gabe. I have you,

and you always tried to see the good in me.

That good is gone, and I'm sorry about that. So sorry. But I was sober until after Jessie was born, so she won't have any problems from her foolish mother.

I wish I listened when I was younger, Gabe. You tried to help. So did your mom, but I couldn't be bothered.

We're going on a run tonight. I don't know how it will end, but Nita promised to bring Jessie to you.

I got these forms online. They give you custody and permission to adopt Jessie, and the free lawyer at the center told me I'd done all the right things. You would be good for her. And I think she would be good for you.

Sister Martha at the mission helped me get some things together that Jessie might need, enough to tide you over for a couple of days.

Please pray for me. This isn't how life was supposed to be, but I've got only myself to blame. And if you can't find it within yourself to raise her, will you find someone who is really nice to do it? I want her surrounded by goodness, and that's not going to happen if she stays with me or my family.

I love you.

Adrianna.

Attached to the two-page letter were official-looking legal documents signed by his cousin Adrianna and witnessed by two people. The stamp of a notary public from Schoharie County indicated that Adrianna had followed the directions of the legal website and the attorney.

"Oh, Gabe." Sympathy deepened Corinne's features. "She sounds like she's in a bad way."

"She's gone, Corinne." He scrubbed a hand to his face, then his neck as the baby slept. "I went to her memorial service two weeks ago, and there were only a handful of us there. Adrianna died while she and her crooked friends were robbing a Thruway exit convenience store. And my mother never said anything about a baby. I can't believe she wouldn't have told me during one of our phone calls."

"Did your mother live near her?" she asked.

"My family is in Saratoga County, on the upper side of Albany. Adrianna got herself mixed up with a bunch of gang members after she dropped out of high school. A wild crowd, according to Mom. She's done time, twice. And now this."

The baby squirmed, stretched and blinked.

"Is there a bottle in there?"

Gabe searched the bag. "No. But there is a can of formula."

"Try the insulated pocket on the side."

He did and withdrew a cool bottle. "How'd you know that was there?"

"Between my two sisters-in-law, I am surrounded by babies. I think all diaper bags have insulated pockets now, but not when I was dragging things around for Tee and Callan."

"Right." He didn't remember that with Gracie's diaper bag, either.

"You might want to heat that quickly, because when she decides she's hungry, she's going to let us know in no uncertain terms."

He remembered that, too, but there was no way Corinne would know he had actual experience because he didn't talk about it. To anyone. Ever.

He hurried to the kitchen, set the bottle in a large coffee mug and filled it with really warm water as he hit Mack's number in his cell phone. He and Susie not only knew Gabe's background, they were familiar with the rough family dynamics. They'd give honest advice. Then he hit 9-1-1, reported what happened and brought the warmed bottle into the living room just as the darkened sky painted an end to their Indian summer day. The wind picked up.

He handed Corinne the bottle because the last thing he was about to do was sit and feed a baby. "I've got to shut the door against that wind."

"I've got this." She lifted Jessie from the carrier as if she did it every day, then snugged her into the crook of her left arm once she settled into his big, broad recliner. She leaned back and stroked the baby's cheek with one slim finger.

The baby turned eagerly. When she found the soft tip of the bottle, she latched on as if it might be her last meal.

"Isn't it amazing, Gabe?"

"Finding an abandoned baby on your doorstep?" Talk about an understatement. "Yes."

"Well, that." She looked at the baby with a smile so sweet and warm that her cool and careful image dissolved before his eyes. "How instinctive we are for survival. God's plan, to nourish us and nurture us. She knows she needs food, she demands it unequivocally, and when she gets full, I bet she smiles up at me to say thank you."

He recalled that oft-played scenario. Gracie's

smile. Her first tear. The way she gripped his finger in the hospital nursery…

He remembered every single moment, which was exactly why there was no way he could ever do it again.

Three cars pulled into his driveway minutes later. Mack and Susie climbed out of the unmarked car and hurried to the door.

Chief of Police Drew Slade and a uniformed officer followed from their respective vehicles.

"Gabe Cutler, what's going on?" Susie kicked off her shoes and crossed to Corinne's side as if magnetized by the sight of such a small baby. "Oh, have you ever seen anything more beautiful?" she whispered softly. "Mack, come see."

Mack raised a questioning brow toward Gabe, then followed Susie. "It's a baby, all right."

Susie jabbed him with her elbow. "It's an amazingly beautiful and wondrous gift from God," she scolded, only half teasing. "And someone left her here, Gabe?"

He waited until Drew was inside, then shared the details.

"I'm not sure of any other particulars," he said, "but it seems we have a situation on our hands."

"Not a situation." The baby fussed and didn't

burp, so Corinne stood and circled the room. She rubbed the tiny girl's back and murmured soft and sweet encouragement. "She's a baby, not a situation. There is a big difference."

"A baby whose presence has caused a situation, then," he acknowledged. Now what on earth was he going to do about it?

"Then Jessie is your cousin, Gabe?" Susie eyed the baby from her spot in the middle of the room, and he'd have to be blind to miss the look of longing in her gaze. She and Mack had been trying for years to have a baby, with no success.

"Well, kind of. Her mother is, so I guess she is, too."

"She's your first cousin once removed," Corinne said softly. "If you have kids someday, she'd be their second cousin. Oh, there," she crooned when the baby let forth a burp far too big for such a tiny child. "Good girl, doesn't that feel so much better?"

The baby pulled her little head back and smiled a big, wide, toothless grin of agreement.

The entire room stood still.

"Oh, Gabe." Susie looked over at him, then Mack. "She is so perfect."

"And I expect she wants the rest of that bottle now," Corinne supposed. "Susie, do you want to feed her?"

"May I?" She exchanged one of those feminine looks with Corinne, the kind men recognize but can never quite comprehend.

"It would be rude of me not to offer," Corinne told her as she laid Adrianna's daughter into Susie's arms. "This way we both get our baby fix."

Susie sank onto the couch and began feeding the baby.

"Well, it is a tough situation." Drew didn't mess around with semantics. "Gabe, she may have left the baby with you but not with your consent, so we're still talking a possible case of child abandonment here. Except with Adrianna gone, the baby becomes a ward of the state, I believe."

"Leaving her with her cousin isn't the same as on a stranger's doorstep." Corinne didn't hesitate to jump in, but then Drew was her brother-in-law. "She had the presence of mind to draw up legal papers countersigned by witnesses and a notary. I think she did way more than most desperate mothers might do under the circumstances. She had a contingency plan when things went bad and had her friend implement the plan, but the mother's intent is clearly defined in these papers." She held up the legal forms Gabe had retrieved from the diaper bag.

"There's protocol, Corinne."

"Drew. Darling." She crossed the room and looped her arm through her brother-in-law's and Gabe knew the chief of police didn't stand a chance. "There is always protocol. And sometimes there are moments when protocol gets bested by common sense. Gabe's cousin did one of the smartest things she could have done for her baby girl. She left her with a man who'll see to her future as long as it takes."

"He'll what?" Gabe stared at her, dismayed. "You mean watch over whoever takes her, right?"

"Takes her?"

The disbelief in his neighbor's eyes should have shamed him, but this wasn't his fault. Adrianna should have known better. She knew his past. Corinne didn't. "She can't stay here, Corinne."

"She can't?"

Mack frowned when Susie tucked the baby closer to her chest. "What are you going to do with her, Gabe?"

Silence reigned.

Corinne stood less than ten feet away. Was she disappointed in him?

Well, join the club because he'd been disappointed in himself for years.

The uniformed officer cleared his throat and Drew withdrew his phone. "I can call Child Protective Services, Gabe. They'll find a foster home for her. They've always got emergency placement homes lined up."

Foster care.

It was a viable alternative. He could drop by and visit the baby, make sure everything was all right. It would give him time to think. Time to rationalize the irrationality of finding babies on doorsteps.

She cooed just then. She leaned back, away from the bottle, and when Gabe looked down, the soft coo of her voice tunneled him back twelve years.

Elise, nursing their baby girl, then Gracie pausing her meal to smile up at him. At her dad. At the man who pledged to keep her safe and sound, all of her days.

He couldn't do this.

He crossed to the door, needing space, needing air, needing—

He barged through to the outside and hauled in a deep breath.

It wasn't enough air, not nearly enough.

A wind gust brought a flutter of last leaves

down around him, gold and red and orange and yellow, spiraling to the ground.

People around town spouted how they loved fall; the parade of colors; the crisp, cold nights; the sun-swept hills of tree-changing splendor.

They were stupid.

The change of colors signified one thing: loss of life. The leaf got one shot at being glorious before being trampled.

Dark thoughts ran through his head. He'd failed before, miserably. How could Adrianna think him good enough to look after such a prize? Such a perfectly wonderful tiny soul?

"Gabe."

He turned.

Corinne stood in the doorway. She beckoned him in.

The cold wind picked up, tossing her hair over her shoulders, into her face.

She'd never understand.

Well, she won't if you don't give her a chance, his conscience reasoned. *She might surprise you because people who've loved and lost are pretty empathetic.*

He saw Drew beyond the window, his phone to his ear.

Susie was holding the baby as if wishing she could change places with him. The young officer stood off to the side, quiet and still, uncertain.

But not as uncertain as Gabe at that moment. He pulled his keys out of his pocket and raised them up. "I'll be back."

"Gabe." She moved across the narrow porch, her arms clutched around her middle. "Come back, Gabe. Please. Drew's making arrangements."

Making arrangements.

Just like that, as if one word from him sealed the baby's fate. Adrianna had offered him a chance—

A chance he didn't dare take.

"Tell him to go ahead. I need time, Corinne. Just…" He settled into his car and backed it out, around Drew's cruiser. And then he drove north, away from the lake, and then west, away from people because the last thing Gabe Cutler wanted to do was fail another innocent child.

Gabe's driveway sat empty when he pulled back into the house two hours later.

Drew had sent him a text shortly after he left the lakeshore. Baby in good hands. Take your time figuring this out. We locked up the house.

They'd left. And they'd taken that sweet, innocent baby with them.

Good.

That was better for her. Better than being in his care.

Is it? his conscience wondered. *Is being with strangers better for Jess? Or better for you?*

He pulled into the drive, shut off the engine and hung his head, ashamed.

He'd run away in that baby's hour of need. What kind of person did that?

A surprised one?

He ignored the mental sensibility. Gabe wasn't about to let himself off that easy. Sure, he was surprised, but it wasn't surprise that sent him scurrying into the hills. It was panic, pure and simple.

The wind swept in from the west, an early glimpse of the coming winter. Leaves spiraled and tumbled in the surrounding darkness, adding touches of color to fading leaf clutter already on the ground.

He parked the car in the garage and climbed out on leaden legs.

Adrianna was gone, but tied up in a swirl of bad choices, she'd tried to do something right. Only it wasn't right. She said she trusted him with her child, but what she messed up—what she couldn't possibly understand—was that he didn't trust himself.

And that made all the difference.

Chapter Five

"Hey, what was going on over at Coach's house today?" Tee asked as she and Corinne cleared the table from dinner. Callan had gone upstairs to write a report due on Monday. "I saw a bunch of cars there, including Uncle Drew's, but then they were all gone by the time I was done with my Revolutionary War project profile. Did they have to move more stuff in?"

Corinne shaded the truth to give Gabe time to figure things out. "A case they'd been working on needed some fine-tuning."

"On a Saturday when he moves into a new house?"

"The law never rests."

"I guess." Tee rinsed the last bowls and tucked them into the dishwasher, then asked a question she hadn't asked in a long while. "Do you still miss my dad?"

Tee never called Dave "Daddy." Was that because she'd never known him, despite Corinne's efforts to create a relationship that didn't exist on a physical level? She didn't know. She swiped a wet cloth to the table and answered as honestly as she could. "Every day. But not like it used to be."

Tee scrunched her brow, waiting for a deeper explanation.

"Your dad and I loved each other. And when he died, my heart just about fell apart. It kind of shattered into a gazillion little pieces, like when the ice breaks apart in the spring."

"Crunching and crackling and groaning."

"Exactly. But then you were born, like the best gift God could have possibly given me." Her words inspired Tee's smile. "Callan was two and I was so busy taking care of both of you that I didn't have time to feel sorry for myself. I missed him like crazy, but then it was more like I missed him because of what you both missed. Hearing him laugh. Hearing him sing."

"Was he a good singer?"

"He was a terrible singer, but he was funny, so we all overlooked it. And he loved you guys so much. And me." She wrung the cloth out over the sink. "There was this big, empty hole in our lives because he was missing, but as you guys got older, it wasn't a hole anymore. It was like a space, growing smaller and smaller because we were filling up our lives with our times. Our memories. Our songs."

"I miss having a dad sometimes."

Tee wasn't the type to wax sentimental often, so Corinne set the washcloth down and waited.

"Not like when you'd expect it." Tee wrinkled her face slightly. "You know like the father-daughter breakfast at church and the father-daughter race for the homeless." Tee liked running races for good causes. She was born to run, fearless and free. Organized sports worked well for Callan, but not for Tee, the classic nonconformist.

"I miss it most when we do normal things. Like moving here. Or when there's a school concert. Or even sometimes in church, when it feels like everyone has a father except me." She didn't sigh or whine. She glanced around as if looking for answers and none came. "I'm glad you and Grandma and Grandpa told me all about him. I'm glad we've got his pictures here. But there's still this feeling when I look around, that something's missing. Something important, even though Grandpa always tries to take Dad's place."

"But it isn't the same, is it?" Corinne kept her voice soft.

"No." Ever pragmatic, Tee raised her shoulders. "But it isn't bad, either, Mom. I don't sit around fussing over it."

Tee didn't sit around, ever.

"But I think of it at the weirdest times, and then I wonder what I've missed. At least Callan got to meet him."

Corinne's throat tightened. Her hands tensed, because even though Callan didn't have any real memories of his dad, he was part of Callan's early reality. Not Tee's. Pictures of Dave with Callan had places of honor in several rooms. None of that existed for her precious daughter. "Your dad didn't have to see you born to love you, Tee. He loved you from the moment that pregnancy test said you were on the way."

"I know." Tee edged away, not wanting to be convinced, or maybe not needing to be convinced. Corinne wasn't sure which it was. Not really. "But it's not the same as having him hold you. Is it?" She set the towel down when the phone rang in the next room. "Shana Moyer is going to Skype with me for our project so I can see what she got done today. I'll take it upstairs." She answered the phone and dashed up to her room, leaving Corinne alone.

Tee talked a lot, but she evaded important subjects on purpose. Corinne had learned to wait for Tee to open up most conversations, but now with puberty, would she have that option on a regular basis?

Not always.

She updated her online calendar while things were quiet, and when Tee came back downstairs nearly an hour later, Corinne pointed out their upcoming schedule. "If we want to have time to put up outside decorations, we've got to jump on it quickly. Otherwise the festival takes over our lives and the weather will turn and we'll be making a big job out of a normal one."

"And we still haven't taken the boat out once this fall, and only four times over the summer."

She didn't have to say that Callan's sports schedule took precedence. Corinne already knew the truth in it. "I know."

Tee didn't pout this time, and Corinne was pretty sure that was worse. She was quietly accepting that her mother didn't prioritize her feelings or needs, and when your mother was the only game in town, that had to bite deeply. "I'm sorry, Tee."

Again, no fuss. No whine. Tee gave her an almost no-reaction look, then headed for the stairs. "I'm going to bed, Mom. See you in the morning."

No kiss good-night.

No hug.

And she wasn't being a brat, she was simply guarding herself from disappointment.

Guilt sideswiped Corinne. She was tied up the next couple of weeks because she'd signed on to run the festival again, but in trying to be a community leader, she was messing up what little time she still had with her daughter.

Callan's baseball team swallowed a huge bunch of family time three seasons a year. Four, if you counted winter workouts.

And all this time Tee had gone along, as if family life centered on Callan. All she'd wanted now that they lived in the lake house was time to enjoy the proximity to the lake. And her mother had been too busy to make that happen.

Lights shone next door as Gabe's car pulled into his driveway, then his garage. She waited, expecting a light to come on inside.

None did.

His house stayed dark.

He was coming home to a shadowed, empty house. Did he know that Drew had asked Kate Gallagher to keep the baby for right now, to give Gabe time? Did he know she was in good hands?

He cared.

She saw that right off, and she saw something more. Much more.

He cared too much, maybe, because when he looked down at that baby, it wasn't just fear that creased worry lines in his face. It was fear mixed with wonder, as if the greatest joy and challenge lay before him.

Lord, help him with whatever this is. Whatever's going on. Help him to come to peace with this, one way or another.

Drew had made an on-the-spot decision to keep the baby out of the system, buying Gabe time. But little Jessie couldn't be left in limbo forever, which meant Gabe needed to make either peace or a decision before too long.

Gabe woke up from a broken sleep possibly more tired than when he lay down. He needed coffee and maybe a run to clear his brain. A few miles of fresh air and a quick pace might help him figure things out. He stepped out of the house with Tucker by his side. Tee's voice hailed him almost instantly.

"Hey, Coach!"

She waved furiously from the deck as she crossed toward the car. She was dressed for church, and while a part of him wanted to take off, he couldn't do it. He paused as she approached, looking vibrant and full of life and love. "Mom said we've got to get going on our outside Christmas stuff today because the weather's supposed to be nice, only we don't have a ladder high enough for over there." Tee pointed to the roofline facing the water. "Everybody that stays for the winter decorates both sides so that folks can see the ring of lights around the water."

Another thing he'd never considered, how a small-town lakeside community would have its holiday traditions even though he'd noticed the lit houses reflected in December waters.

"It's really beautiful to see," Tee added. "Do you have a taller ladder at your house?"

Christmas lights. Decorations. No place to run, nowhere to hide. That reality broadsided Gabe as he faced his excited young neighbor. "In the garage, hanging on the wall."

"Tee. I told you not to bother Coach." Corinne came out of the house just then. She had her purse over her shoulder and keys clutched in her hand, clearly in a hurry. "Grandpa has a tall ladder. I'm sure he'll be happy to bring it over." She faced Gabe and he saw it again, the concern he'd read in her eyes the day before. "Each season I discover something else I didn't realize I'd need living down here. The tall ladder is only the latest item. My grandfather didn't hang lights from the roof, but the kids love them."

"My ladder is right here." He pointed backward. "No sense bothering Pete to come over."

"That's actually a good point," Corinne noted before she called out Callan's name. She moved toward the car as Callan appeared on the deck steps. "Pete's doing great since his cancer treatment, but he suffers from vertigo if he's up too high. If he brings the ladder, he'll want to do the upper reaches himself. I'm not after a trip to the ER today."

"And Coach said we can borrow his," Tee reminded her.

"Then thank you, Gabe. We'll grab it after church." She made no mention of yesterday's drama, and drove off with the kids as if it was all normal.

It wasn't normal, and he didn't like people knowing that.

He'd traded the anonymity of being in a small house on a farm-friendly country road for this spot on the water, next door to people who knew him as well as anyone from Grace Haven. He'd kept his life private, purposely, but now…here…doors of silence were being wrenched open.

He took the first mile too fast.

Not for Tucker. The tricolored collie mix

took everything in stride, unlike his owner. And by the time they finished mile three, not knowing what had happened with Adrianna's baby was driving him crazy. He texted Drew when he and Tucker got back from the run. How is Jessie? Can I see her?

Drew texted back quickly. Tucked in temporary care. Doing fine. And yes. On my way to church right now. Is later okay?

Gabe typed quickly. Yes.

The house felt emptier when they returned. The unlikelihood of that weighed on him, because the house was the same as it had been when he bought it a few weeks before.

And yet different, somehow, because there'd been a baby here, as if she belonged here. She didn't, of course. And yet…

Tucker nuzzled his snout beneath Gabe's hand, and then he went to the door and cocked one ear, as if asking a question.

Stop thinking about it. If this was a police case, how would you handle it?

Only he couldn't relegate it to impersonal status.

He looked next door.

What did Corinne think of him? Of his behavior? His reaction?

It shouldn't matter what she thought, but

something in her expression made him think she might understand.

Well, she can't if you don't talk about it. And you never talk about it.

He hit his mother's number on his cell phone. The call went straight to voice mail.

Agitation spiked his pulse. He didn't like things in flux. He liked to know what was happening, and when, every single day. He didn't consider himself regimented. He was... orderly.

Think. Pray. And maybe giving yourself over to God's plans would be a good start.

He carried the ladder next door so he could lock the house, then gathered his fishing gear. Yesterday's cold blast had mellowed to a soft, fall day. He'd take the boat out, drop a line and think things through. He liked praying in church most times, but nothing beat a man, a lake and a solid-grip fishing pole.

Corinne stretched from the upper rungs, trying to loop as many feet of lights as she could without climbing down and moving the ladder, but when it began to list with her at the top, she was really glad the porch roof kept the whole thing from skidding to the ground.

"Come down from there. Please."

She turned, startled by Gabe's deep voice. "Gabe. You scared me. I didn't see you come back."

"Well, I did just in time to see this ladder almost fall over. Come down, there're plenty of things to do at ground level. I'll do this."

She shook her head instantly. "Don't be silly. I've got this, I—"

He stared up at her. The look on his face managed to erase any form of rational thought. She didn't dare let that become a regular occurrence, but how could she stop it with him living next door? He kept his voice softer now, but not much. "Please? My arms are longer."

They were, and she knew she'd been stretching the limits by leaning so far to the left... "Are you sure?"

"Yes."

Finally she climbed down. He held the ladder firm until she was on the ground, then he hoisted it. "I should have offered to do this for you earlier. I'm sorry I didn't."

"Gabe, it's fine. We don't expect you to jump in on every crazy family project we do, and this..." Corinne indicated the various lighted projects with a wince. "This is what happens when you combine my grandparents' decorations with ours and Tee wants to use every single one."

"Sounds like Tee."

"Or a *National Lampoon* movie," Corinne muttered. "But they're growing up so fast that I hate to say no over something like this."

"Do you want the lights to wrap the porch posts, too?"

"If you don't mind."

"Got it."

He didn't say anything about yesterday's events. Neither did she. As she helped organize the resin nativity set, a group of lighted reindeer, two inflatable Charlie Brown and Snoopy scenes from her grandfather's favorite Christmas special and cord after cord of twinkle lights, Tee's chatter and Christmas music filled the air with promise of the upcoming holiday season.

Gabe worked, eyes forward, focused and silent.

He didn't sing. He didn't smile. He didn't join in Tee's chatter.

Tucker sat at the base of the ladder, looking up. He wagged his tail whenever Gabe glanced down, and even a firm curmudgeon couldn't ignore the dog's obvious affection. And when Callan called Tucker over for a game of Frisbee catch midday, the dog didn't move. He stayed right by Gabe's side until his master's work was done.

"Such loyalty deserves a reward, my friend." Corinne slipped Tucker a piece of sliced ham, then petted his shaggy head. "You're such a good boy."

"He is." Gabe tipped the ladder down, then balanced it carefully from the middle.

"Coach, I'll help you carry it back." Callan took the front end without being asked. "Mom made sandwiches and the one o'clock game started half an hour ago. Wanna watch it with us?"

"Wish I could, but I've got some things to take care of this afternoon."

"Oh. Yeah. Sure." Callan fumbled the words, as if embarrassed he'd had the audacity to ask. His quieter nature meant he didn't put himself out there like his younger sister, so he wasn't as accustomed to rejection.

"Next week?" Gabe's question smoothed what could have been an awkward moment, and Corinne blessed him for it. "I'll be ready to relax over a game once the festival is over."

Callan's eyes lit up. "That would be great."

"Is that all right with you, Corinne?"

What choice did she have? It wasn't a date. It was a neighbor, coming by for football and nachos. "Sounds good. I'll put a pot of something on and we can just relax for the afternoon." That was what she said, but the thought of relaxing around Gabe Cutler was an impossibility. But that was her problem. Not his.

His phone rang after they'd rehung the ladder. He took the call and paced toward the water, talking quietly. And when he disconnected the call, he stayed where he was, staring at the calm, thin stretch of Canandaigua Lake, unmoving.

"Coach, I can't wait to try the lights tonight! Our first Christmas on the water and so many decorations! Isn't it the coolest ever?"

Quiet moments of grave introspection were brief when Tee was around. She raced across the yard and seized Gabe's hand. "Won't it be beautiful?"

He looked down, as if he couldn't help himself. Did Tee recognize the pain in his face?

Probably not, but her mother did. Gabe looked at Tee, then the house. He tried to smile, but it was more of a grimace. "Sure will."

"And I'm turning every radio station we have to the Christmas channel," she declared, still wringing the big guy's hand.

"Tee, it's not even Thanksgiving yet," Callan protested as he stowed a box of supplies in the back of their detached garage. "Give us a break, okay?"

"If we weren't supposed to listen, the radio station wouldn't play them all day. But I'll leave yours alone," she added as if being magnanimous. "Mostly because you'll kill me if I mess with your stuff."

Callan laughed. "Glad we see eye-to-eye on that." A car pulled into the driveway to drop off two of Tee's friends. Callan made a pretend face of fear, and headed for the house. "Family room is off-limits to girls during football if they giggle and talk like you do."

"Worse than me, by far," Tee promised him, then laughed. "See ya, Coach! Thanks for helping!"

She ran to greet her friends, and then they disappeared into the house, too, leaving Corinne with Gabe. She crossed the driveway to thank him. "I appreciate the help, Gabe."

His jaw firmed. He glanced from decoration to decoration, almost grim. "It's okay."

Not "happy to help" or "glad to do it," and that was all right, because Corinne was pretty sure he wasn't happy to do it. And yet he had.

"Coffee?"

That perked his interest, but then he surprised her by pointing at his place. Not hers. "Drew's coming by in a few minutes."

If ever a man looked like he bore the weight

of the world on his shoulders, it was her new neighbor. "With the baby?"

"Yes." He didn't sound one bit resolved. "I haven't heard back from my mother. I don't know if she's aware of any of this, but I can't leave it like this. Babies don't belong in limbo. They belong somewhere. With someone."

She believed that, too. "Then coffee at your place sounds good to me." She didn't ask if he'd made any decisions. It wasn't her business. But she'd dealt with parents in crisis and grief far too many times over the years, and Gabe Cutler fit the profile.

Whatever he chose—whatever he decided— she prayed it might relieve some of the angst he tried so hard to hide. Angst that seemed to go far deeper than a thirtysomething bachelor, trying to live his life. And how did she know this?

Because she was guilty of the very same thing.

Chapter Six

Drew pulled into Gabe's driveway a quarter hour later. Pete and Kate Gallagher followed him into the drive. Once Pete parked the car, Gabe realized why.

Pete and Kate had Jessie with them.

His heart sped up as Kate lifted the baby carrier from the car seat base. His hands flexed. His palms went damp. He swung the door wide. Pete caught it on his side, then stepped back for Kate to come through. "You kept her overnight?" Gabe wasn't sure what to say. How to react. He was used to being the one taking care of things. Not the one being helped. "Thank you."

"Kept things simple," Pete said. "If we're doing a friend a favor by babysitting, county protocol becomes a non-issue."

"I'm grateful, sir." He was, too, because once

legal wheels got rolling, putting the brakes on was next to impossible. "I want to apologize for taking off yesterday."

"None needed," Drew told him. "And Pete and Kate have offered to babysit longer if you need them to step in."

Kind people. Caring people. The Gallaghers reached out to help others all the time. Only Gabe wasn't used to getting help, or accepting it.

Corinne undid the car seat straps and lifted the baby from the seat as Mack and Susie's car rolled into his driveway. They'd stayed by his side through thick and thin and they understood his mixed emotions better than anyone.

"Hey, precious. How are you?" Corinne nuzzled the baby's soft cheek. "Oh, I could just eat you up, you are that sweet!"

"She's happy for the moment because she downed a full six ounces just before we came over," Kate offered. "She loves to eat, and that's never a bad thing, is it, Shnookums?"

"A good appetite is a wonderful thing in a baby." Corinne blew bubbly kisses against the baby's cheek, laughing, then drew back, totally relaxed, and Gabe had another flash of intuition.

Corinne didn't relax often. Not fully, anyway. Another trait they shared. But here, holding a baby, he glimpsed the tender woman within her.

The baby's face split into a wide smile. She opened her mouth, staring up at Corinne, and tried to smile wider but couldn't. It was...adorable.

"Are you just so happy to be here?" Corinne cooed the words gently, still smiling.

Jessie batted her hands. She kicked her feet, cooing soft sounds that sure sounded like she was happy to be here.

His heart stretched open, watching.

What if Adrianna hadn't made her arrangements ahead of time? What if she'd left this baby with whomever? Then Jessie would be a cog in the system. If she even made it to the system.

"Your cousin went to great lengths to find a safe place for her baby." Drew stated the truth in a matter-of-fact voice as Susie and Mack slipped in through the front door. "She might have been over the edge, but she jumped through a lot of hoops to make sure Jessie would be cared for. The ball's in your court, Gabe. We can have the county step in if that's what you want, but if you need more time, we can do that for you."

Could he actually hand this baby over to Child Protective Services? Turn his back on her?

No.

But did he trust himself enough to care for her?

His pulse increased. A cool sweat broke out on his neck. The room felt cold and hot, all at once.

Serious discussion paused when Tee raced through the back door, skidded to a stop and whistled like a pro. "Who's under arrest? The baby?" she teased as she crossed the room to where Corinne had Jessie snugged in the curve of her arm. "Are you a hardened criminal?" She spoke in a baby-friendly voice. She leaned down into the baby's face, and when Jessie burbled up at her and smiled, Tee burst out laughing. "Uncle Drew, you can't arrest her unless the charge is too cute for her own good. Can I hold her?"

Corinne said yes before Gabe could utter a word. "Of course. Have you washed your hands?"

"Just did. We made PB&J with marshmallow fluff and I was pretty sticky." Tee reached out and lifted the baby from her mother.

Gabe moved forward to explain how she needed to support the baby's head, and to hang on tight, and not to slip on the floor in her sock-clad feet.

Tee turned, one hand behind the baby's bald

head, the other supporting the lower end like a pro. "Oh, she is the sweetest thing, isn't she, Mom? I love being surrounded by babies now! It was like forever since I was born, and no babies in all that time, and now with all the aunts getting married, we seem to have babies and cute little kids everywhere."

Corinne's phone jangled an upbeat song in Tee's pocket. "Oops, Mom, someone's been trying to get you. That's why I ran over here. And to see what all the commotion was about, of course." She grinned in admission. "Here." In total tween nonchalance, she passed Jessie to Gabe before she withdrew the phone and handed it to her mother.

Maybe if he held on tight and didn't look down, it would be all right.

If he just—

Too late.

He looked down.

Wide blue eyes looked back at him. Blue eyes surrounded by fair lashes and a pale head with just a whisper of hair.

Oh, his heart...

She reached up. Touched his chin. The bristle made her face scrunch, as if wondering why he felt rough.

He felt rough because he was rough, inside

and out, but when he breathed in the scent of her, a hint of baby powder and baby soap…

He was hooked. Mesmerized.

He reached out a finger.

She grasped it, quick as a wink, folding a tiny hand around his big pointer finger as if holding on forever.

His heart clenched tight, then began to ease as if it had been waiting for this moment a long, long time. It opened just enough for him to say, "We won't be needing a place for her." He took a deep breath, a big, deep breath, then lifted his gaze to Drew's. "It seems she's got a place. Right here."

The room seemed to breathe again.

"Consider it done," Drew said. "We're set for the moment. I'll follow through with the report on our end. We'll have to let Saratoga know what's gone on."

"Let's hold off on telling Adrianna's parents about this," Gabe said. "They're quite rigid, and wanted nothing to do with their daughter or this child. They've kept themselves estranged from most of the family for years. I want to keep it from them just long enough for me to talk with my mother."

Corinne had reentered the room while he was talking. "The letter said they wanted nothing to do with the baby," she reminded them.

"I think that's grounds for keeping things quiet for a bit. At least long enough for Gabe to do some checking."

"I'll advise Saratoga, but it will be their call. Still…" Drew shrugged. "They'll probably be glad to let us handle things here because the baby's here."

"Where will she sleep?" asked Corinne.

"We put our extra portable crib in the back of the SUV, just in case," said Kate. "And Emily sent a bag of baby girl clothes over. They need a quick washing because they've been in storage."

A crib. Baby clothes from Kate and Pete's middle daughter. A new reality emerging…

"And I got a box of diapers and an extra can of formula last night, so we have the important bases covered." Drew made the baseball analogy with a knowing grin, and he was right. Food and diapers were two very important things when it came to babies.

Gabe swallowed hard. "That's great. I'll grab some money from my—"

"I don't want your money," Drew cut in. He waved Gabe off. "Keep it to buy her something pretty. Pretend this is a baby shower and that's my gift. Pete and I will get the crib and the clothes for you."

"Where should we set it up?" asked Mack. "Down here or upstairs?"

Gabe hesitated, then pointed to the living room. "Here is good. Closer to bottles. I can sleep on the couch until we've got some kind of schedule worked out."

"Nothing like a baby to set their own schedule." Kate sounded downright cheerful about the whole thing.

"Coaching is done for now, so that's good." Corinne's sensibility helped him see the positive side of this timing. "No extra-long days or weekends away. What about child care while you're working?"

"I'm off on Monday. That will give me time to check things out."

"Sounds good." Drew lifted a hand in farewell. "I'm heading out. I told Kimberly I'd get some outside stuff done while the weather cooperates. We'll talk soon, Gabe." He moved toward the door.

"Drew."

The chief of police paused.

"Thanks."

Drew acknowledged that with a quiet look. "It's all right."

Gabe snugged Jessie farther into the curve of his arm. She pulled his finger toward her mouth, gave him a toothless grin, then yawned, clutching his rusty heart a little firmer with each baby move. She yawned again, in earnest. "Ready for a nap, little lady? How about a fresh diaper first?"

"Right here." Corinne handed him a diaper from the bag. "Would you like me to change her?"

"I've got it."

He settled her down on the cushioned carpet and undid a puzzle's worth of snaps. When he had the new diaper in place, she scowled and batted tiny hands at his face.

"She says you're slow."

He almost laughed, then winced instead. "She's right. This stuff takes practice."

"Gabe, I've got some unused vacation." Susie moved two steps closer. "I could watch her for a week or two. Give you time to get used to things."

Susie would be great with her. He knew that. But what if she grew too attached?

He glimpsed Mack's frown behind her, as if he worried about the same thing. "Susie, can I put that offer on hold? Let me get my bearings, but there could be times when I need you and I don't want to wear out my welcome this quick."

"Of course." She tried to smile, and remorse hit him square.

Why was such a nice couple denied the chance to be parents and an irresponsible young woman like Adrianna given a perfectly gorgeous child? He had no answers, only more questions. He didn't want this surprise baby to drive a wedge between him and two dear friends. But he didn't feel right accepting Susie's quick offer, either, because he wasn't blind to the longing in her voice. The hope in her eyes. He'd been praying daily for a healthy baby for them because he understood their round of losses far too well.

"Rory has contacts with several local day care facilities," Pete said.

Rory was a regular at Callan's baseball games, enthusiastic, funny and recently married with two adopted children who were quickly becoming ardent baseball fans. "She's got the preschool at the vineyard south of town, right?"

Corinne nodded. "Casa Blanca. I'm sure she can hook you up with someone who's got an opening for a baby."

"Can you have her call me later?" He hated to hurt Susie's feelings, but what if this whole thing got messed up once Adrianna's parents found out he had their granddaughter in Grace Haven? He'd be wrong to pile more anxiety on Susie's already full plate.

"I'll text her right now," said Kate. "She'll be glad to help."

Gabe didn't look up. He couldn't. If he did, he'd recognize the hurt he put on his good friend's face.

Tee had taken Tucker over to meet her friends. In typical Tee fashion, she bounded back into the room. "So fill me in! Whose baby are we watching? And can I help? And how long is she here for?"

Tee's entrance offered a welcome interruption to the awkward exchange. Susie put a hand on his shoulder. "Gabe, I think you've got this under control. We're going to head out. Call if you need anything, okay?"

The tremor in her voice made him nod without making eye contact. "Absolutely. And thank you for running right over, guys."

Mack clapped him on the other shoulder. "That's what friends are for. See you Tuesday at work."

"Will do."

Tee slipped onto the floor. "No toys?" She peeked into the diaper bag and frowned. "This is totally wrong by anyone's standards. Mom, we should bring that bag of toys over that we get out for babies."

"You head back to your friends and I'll get the bag while I check the pot of tomato sauce."

"Great! I'm starved!" She darted out, closed the door snugly and dashed next door.

Corinne touched the baby's cheek. "She's precious, Gabe."

"Yes."

"And Susie told me they've been trying to have a baby for a long time with no success. She said that's why she can't just relax and enjoy her pregnancy like a normal person would, because they've all ended the same way. Sadly."

"I know." His jaw went tight. "And it would be an easy answer one way, wouldn't it?" He looked up and met her gaze. He read sympathy and understanding in her troubled look. "But then what if something weird happens? What if the court denies me custody, or Adrianna's parents contest it and I have to give her to them? I can't imagine putting her and Mack through that."

"I agree totally. But I saw how hard it was on you and I wanted you to know I think you're a very special man to do this."

He wasn't one bit special. Not in his estimation. "I'm not special, Corinne." He said the words firmly. "I'm barely good by some standards. And just all right by others."

"You're wrong." She laid a cool, soft hand against his cheek, and the gentle touch made him look up. "Whatever it is that makes you feel that way is wrong, too. But at this moment, the pragmatic task of dinner calls me back to my kitchen. And consider this an invite because there's plenty of sauce and meatballs to go around."

He hadn't bothered with food the night before. And he'd never given it consideration this morning, so the thought of a home-cooked meal sounded better than good. It sounded wonderful.

His life had changed instantly, much like the fall weather. He'd been trudging along, minding his own business and then…

Jessie cooed from the floor. She dimpled, writhed, frowned, then burped. And then she dimpled again, smiling at him.

He couldn't do this. He knew that. And yet—he couldn't not do it, either.

Once the house cleared he'd call his mother and discern what she knew, but for now…

He sank onto the floor while Kate started

a load of baby laundry and Pete wrestled the crib into a more usable state.

For now, he'd sit and marvel at the tiny blessing cooing on the floor before him.

Chapter Seven

Don't get attached, not to the cop or the baby.

The mental warning repeated itself every time Corinne thought about the abandoned baby in Gabe's living room.

Her job brought her face-to-face with a full spectrum of situations and lots of parents, some good, some bad. She'd witnessed young mothers as they gave their newborns up for adoption, and she'd witnessed grievously sad pregnancies gone wrong.

But much of her workload brought happy endings to scared parents facing medical trauma. She clung to that reality during dark days.

She'd just finished arranging hot garlic bread on a platter when Gabe walked through her lakeside door. "Kate commandeered the baby, and I thought you might need some help."

"Your timing is perfect." He looked pained when she said that, but there wasn't time to delve. Not when freshly cooked pasta and sizzling garlic bread was involved. She laid a sheet of aluminum foil over the bread and tucked the ends as Pete followed Gabe through the door.

"Mom said I should make myself useful, but I think she was just trying to get rid of us so Jessie would fall asleep," he announced. He leaned the door shut. "It's getting colder out there. If it frosts tonight, we'll say goodbye to the last leaves."

"And hello to the holidays and snow and the festival," added Corinne. "Gabe, can you set those plates on the table? The girls were recording their harmonic version of 'Santa Claus Is Coming to Town' upstairs, and I promise you that we're all better off with them up there and Tee's door closed."

He set the plates onto the table, then the bread. He glanced around as if worried. About the house? The girls? The baby? Germs?

She wished she could tell him it would all be all right…to relax, let go and "let God," a favorite saying in the Gallagher house, but she understood the reality too well. He'd just been handed an unexpected and very precious situation to handle on his own. She understood that scenario better than most. It would take a dull-witted person to miss the struggle on his face. In his bearing. The verse she loved came to her, telling and true. "There is a time for every purpose under the heaven."

Brave words from the book of Ecclesiastes.

She tried to live the simplicity of the verse, but it wasn't easy. Her faith had been thrown a challenge when Dave died. She'd felt bereft and alone, watching his metal coffin be lowered into the ground, a toddler clutching one hand while pregnant.

What purpose had Dave's death served? She saw the downsides. No, scratch that, she *lived* them, but if everything had a purpose, what reason was there in a young officer's death?

None that she knew of, and that reality challenged the wise words.

"Have we got everything we need?" Pete asked as she set the large bowl of meatballs and sauce in the center of the island.

"I think so. The kids can serve themselves at the island and that frees up some room at the table."

"Corinne."

"Yes, Gabe?"

He moved toward the door. "I know this will sound like I'm being overprotective, but I'm going to keep Jessie over at the house for now. She's little and with so many kids around…"

A shout from one of Tee's girlfriends punctuated the air, and his voice trailed off.

"That's not being overprotective," she told him. "It's smart. I'm not a big fan of dragging tiny babies who haven't had all their shots out into public all the time. Let's let them build up some resistance. And it will give the two of you time to get to know one another. But give me two minutes to dish you up some supper. From one neighbor to another." She dished up pasta and sauce into a plastic container and handed it to him, calm and cool.

"Here's bread, too." Pete hadn't bothered with anything as civilized as a knife. He'd torn off a man-sized hunk of bread and wrapped it in a piece of foil. "I'll walk over with you. It might take two of us to pry Kate away from that baby."

"I'd appreciate the help, sir." He turned at the door and lifted the container. "Thanks for this."

"We're even," she said lightly, not looking his way, because that's how they needed to leave things. Neighborly. Nothing more. Nothing less. "Thanks for helping with the lights. Hey, guys!" She focused her attention upstairs and not on the handsome man standing in her kitchen. "Dinner's ready."

"Coming!"

"Great!"

Callan came up from the family room while Tee and her two friends dashed down from upstairs, and when Corinne turned around, Pete and Gabe were crossing the deck.

She watched them go.

Gabe touched something inside her. A longing or yearning she couldn't afford to let happen. And when Tee, Callan and the other girls had slipped into the chairs she'd placed around the table, she saw validation for her concerns in her children's faces.

They were too young to know what they'd lost twelve years before. She knew. And it was her job to make sure they never had to go through that again.

Once Tee's friends were picked up by their parents, she popped through the hedge. She wasn't dashing over to help, but to make sure that Gabe knew help was available, if needed. She tapped on his side door. When it swung open, he looked surprised and pleased to see her. "Supper was great. Best meatballs I've ever had."

"Going without food for a day might have

shaded your opinion my way, but I'll take the compliment as given. Listen, I'm not interfering…"

"That's what people say when they're about to interfere," Gabe cut in. "It's like saying 'It's not about the money' when of course it's absolutely about the money."

She laughed lightly. "Fair enough. I figured I'd come by and collect my container and remind you that I'm right next door. If you need my help with the baby overnight, I'll have my phone by the bed. Or if you want to do shifts, Gabe." She turned to face him. "I'll be glad to help."

Did she sense the gut-clenching fear inside at the thought of being left alone, responsible for an infant's well-being? She seemed to, and that understanding helped lighten his load.

"You'll be fine. Babies aren't as scary or as fragile as they look."

He knew that wasn't true. He'd known ultimate failure once.

His heart knotted, but what could he do? He'd already refused Susie's offer of help, and that would have been an easily justifiable lifeline, except he couldn't put her in that position. He'd broken enough hearts in his time.

"Call if you need me." She lifted her phone as a reminder. "I'll come running."

"I will."

She slipped out, sent him a quick salute and crossed their connected yards. He watched her disappear inside, then stood there, disjointed, staring at nothing until a peep brought his attention around.

Jessie had rolled over. She had both hands stuffed into her little mouth, peeking up at him with just enough interest that he figured he better mix a couple of bottles ahead of time.

His hands shook.

He breathed deep, through his nose, wanting them to stop.

They didn't, and when he sloshed the first bottle onto the countertop, he righted it and gripped the counter edge so tightly that his knuckles strained white.

He wouldn't be able to sleep.

How could he?

Responsibility rose like a Saturday matinee monster, all-consuming.

He breathed again, released the counter and got two bottles ready before she set up a fuss. He put one in the fridge and brought the other over to the living room.

He needed noise. Something to make it seem

like he wasn't here, alone with his greatest fear, a needy child.

She fussed a little louder, announcing her growing impatience.

He clicked on the Sunday night football game, then crossed the room to the patterned Pack 'n Play. He looked down.

Sky blue eyes stared up at him, round and wide. She looked worried.

Well, that made two of them.

She batted little arms as if wondering what was taking him so long. Then her lower lip trembled slightly, leaving him no choice.

He bent low and picked her up.

So light.

So small.

So precious.

Adrenaline rushed through his system.

He shoved it aside.

Every self-preservation instinct he'd been honing for nine years told him to run next door, hand this baby to Corinne and head for the hills.

Of course he couldn't do that because Adrianna had trusted him to oversee things. Small matter that her judgment was obviously twisted.

He snugged Jessie into his left arm in a hold he'd never forgotten and adjusted her bottle.

She drank eagerly, fists bound tight as if worried that food might not arrive on time. He muted the TV, turned his phone on speaker and called his mother. If anyone knew the background story, it would be Linda Cutler. This time the call went right through.

"Gabe, hey!"

Her voice made the baby lurch, and he fumbled to turn the phone volume down.

"You never call on a Sunday night. What's up?"

"Mom, did you know that Adrianna had a child?"

She sighed and went quiet. For long seconds the only sound was the baby's murmurs of growing contentment as she slurped a bottle in what might be record time. "Yes, I knew. She'd gone to an agency to give the baby up for adoption in her last trimester, and then I heard nothing. I'm sure the baby's in good hands with a family longing for a child. We have to commend her for that."

"Did Aunt Maureen and Uncle Blake know she was pregnant?"

"Yes."

"And they did nothing to help?"

"They'd given up on her, Gabe. They didn't want her or that baby around. They considered the thought of the baby a culmination of sin. They made that quite clear."

Anger rose within him. He was thirteen years older than Adrianna, and they hadn't known each other well, but Gabe was pretty sure her parents had given up on the girl a long time ago. "Who does that, Mom? Who gives up on a kid because they've made mistakes? She'd been clean for nearly two years."

"Maureen and Blake have strict beliefs."

He knew that, but didn't Christ forgive sinners? Didn't he bring the outsiders into his realm purposely?

"I told Adrianna I'd be glad to help her, but she sent me a nice note about the agency, then disappeared. And that's all I knew until..." She sighed again and when she spoke, her voice went thick with regret. "Until she was gone."

The image of his younger cousin, who'd tried to straighten herself out after a two-year stint in women's prison, haunted him.

"How did you find out, Gabe? I've never said anything to anyone, and I can't imagine Maureen and Blake are talking about it."

"I found out because someone dropped off a four-month-old baby girl on my doorstep yesterday afternoon. She came with a handful of diapers and an envelope of custody papers tucked into a diaper bag."

"That can't be." He could almost see his mother standing, pacing. "She was giving the baby up for adoption. She told me her plan and it didn't include robbing places at gunpoint with a baby. Gabe, are you sure?"

He glanced down at the baby girl snugged into the crook of his arm. "Reasonably certain. I'm giving her a bottle right now. Her note said she didn't want strangers to have her baby. So she chose me. You really didn't know that she hadn't given up the baby?"

"No. I'm sure no one knew. Oh, Gabe." She sighed softly. "Wait until her parents hear this. They wanted nothing to do with their own daughter when she was less than perfect, and the thought that they could put those demands on another generation is scary, isn't it? My sister was never cut out to be a mother, I'm afraid."

He frowned, confused by her assumption that his aunt and uncle would want—and be awarded—guardianship of Jessie. "Why would they get custody?" he asked bluntly. "Adrianna clearly signed the baby over to me, complete with witnesses and a notary." Jessie blinked up at him. A tiny dribble of milk ran out of the corner of her mouth, and when he dabbed it away with a soft towel, oh, that smile!

His heart softened, and his resolve firmed

up. "Mom, there's no way Aunt Maureen and Uncle Blake are getting their hands on this baby. They don't know she's here. They don't know where she is, and I don't think they care."

"But we'll have to tell them," she said softly. "It's the right thing to do."

Was it?

Gabe wasn't so sure, and the whole thing was too new to figure out right now. "Well, they don't need to know right away. I've got enough on my plate right now."

"I can come help."

He'd like that, actually. His mother had always been a voice of common sense in the middle of her crazy family dynamics. "Can you come next weekend? We've got the Christkindl festival, and I'm working the whole three days. If you could drive up here and take charge of Jessie, that would be wonderful."

"Jessie. That's her name?"

"Jessica Anne, according to the birth certificate, but Adrianna called her Jessie in the letter. She's beautiful, Mom."

"Of course she is." She sighed. "I'll come Friday morning and spend the weekend. But you need to think about telling your aunt and uncle. At some point," she added softly.

He would, but not now. Not yet. "I will. But the thought that they might fight for custody and mess up her life…" He passed a hand over the nape of his neck, then brought the baby up for a burp as naturally as if he'd been doing these things right along. "I can't wrap my head around that, Mom."

"We'll talk next weekend. And we'll pray, Gabe. For you, for this baby—and for guidance."

He could use prayer for all of the above. "Thanks, Mom. I've got to go, she needs a diaper change."

"All right. I'll call tomorrow to see how things are going. Are you okay with this, Gabe?" He sensed the hesitation in her voice. "I mean really okay?"

He wasn't, but worrying his mother didn't cut it. "Fine. Yes."

"Then I'll talk to you tomorrow. I can't say this was the phone call I ever expected to get, but there's a part of me that's proud of what Adrianna did. She took steps to ensure her baby's well-being in the thick of poor choices. For all of her faults, that shows a mother's love."

"It does. Good night, Mom."

"Good night, son."

He stood and paced the room, patting the baby's back.

She belched, then brought her head around

to smile at him, thoroughly pleased with herself.

A text came in. He looked at the phone. Call or text if you need me. Walking that baby around the living room might get old around 1 a.m.

He moved toward the window.

Corinne was silhouetted in her living room window, watching him. She waved, and he waved back, suddenly not as alone.

He texted back, Appreciate it. Thanks.

You're welcome, came the reply.

Her window went dark, but knowing she was there, ready to help, meant more than being a good neighbor.

It meant everything.

Chapter Eight

Corinne got home midday Monday.

She hadn't heard from Gabe during the night. Had things gone well? She hoped so.

She needed to check on him.

Needed or wanted?

Both, she decided. She'd grabbed a submarine sandwich at the deli. A man who moves into a new house, then gets a baby dropped on his doorstep, all within twenty-four hours, probably didn't have time to shop for groceries. She tapped lightly. He swung open the door, looking positively haggard. She frowned in understanding and sympathy. "No sleep, huh?"

"An hour. Once. She's got her day and night reversed, as you can see."

She peeked around him and spied the baby curled up, sound asleep in the portable crib. Tucker lay nearby, also sound asleep. She redirected her attention up to Gabe. He looked done in, and she remembered those times too well. She thrust the sandwich into his plans and walked in. "So here's the plan."

"Don't wake her, Corinne." He made a mock-desperate face that was probably more real than fake. He added a pretend growl, as if ready to stand his ground. "For the love of all that's good and holy, don't wake her."

She almost laughed out loud but caught herself just in time because she understood the joy of a sleeping baby. "I'm going to babysit right now so you can sleep. I'll take Jessie to my place, so you can relax."

Yesterday he had refused offers of help. A sleepless night managed to change his tune. "You wouldn't mind?"

Mind? Not in the least, but if she sounded too anxious he'd hear the ticktock of her rusting biological clock. "I'd love it. And you'll feel better after some rest. Why didn't you call me last night?"

"Guilt. I kept thinking of how nice it is to get a good night's sleep, and it felt mean to wake you up. And I knew you had to work today, so I persevered."

"I'm on half days today and tomorrow because of the festival, then I took vacation for the rest of the week. And when someone makes you an offer of help, the right thing to do is take them up on that offer. Which means you should have called. But I do understand, because I was the same way, always insisting I could do everything myself. I was a single-parent dork. I kind of still am." She couldn't believe she was admitting that out loud, but she just did. "I'm not exactly proud of it."

"I don't think you're a dork, Corinne."

That voice. The look, as if he understood more than he possibly could.

"I can own it," she admitted. "Right now I'm going to enjoy an afternoon with this sweet baby while you rest. Got it?" She lifted the sleeping infant and wrapped her in a blanket. "Can you hook me up with a couple of bottles and diapers?"

"Gratefully."

He looked done in. Worn out. But she sensed strength, too. Strength from within.

She wanted to reach up a hand. Touch his tired cheek. Assure him everything would be okay.

But she couldn't do that and maintain her strict boundaries. His living so close had already messed up her strictly from-a-distance policy when it came to Gabe Cutler.

His being next door and needing help with a four-month-old baby turned the tables completely.

A baby changes everything... The words of the country song came back to her, a beautiful ballad of the first Christmas, still true today. A baby *did* change everything, which meant she had to harden her heart and stand firm. As she crossed the yard, she didn't try to pretend it would be easy. Because the stakes had gone up. Way up.

He followed her into the house. She tucked the baby onto the quilt she'd spread on the floor. Jessie wriggled, sighed, then latched onto her pacifier and dozed back off.

"That's what I call an excellent transfer of goods," she said softly as she stood. "Transporting sleeping children without waking them is a highly desired parenting skill. Phase one of Operation Gabe Sleeps is complete."

His hand on her shoulder made her pause, and then turn.

"This means a lot to me, Corinne." His gaze went from her to the baby, and she sensed more than fatigue behind his words. "I'll be able to relax, knowing she's in good hands."

"Good." This time she did reach up and touch his cheek.

He leaned into her touch, then smiled.

Her heart went crazy.

Her pulse fluttered in a way that couldn't possibly be good for either of them, but it didn't just feel *good*.

It felt marvelous. She withdrew her hand from his stubbly cheek. "See you later."

He didn't hurry across the yard like she expected.

He walked, eyes down, but when he got to his yard, he turned, looking tired but focused, too. He spotted her in the window and waved. And then he smiled.

The smile brightened everything. The angst of his cousin's life, the crush of festival prep, the gray November day...

Amazing how one sincere smile helped make everything seem more doable. She loved his smile. That frank grin had attracted her over two years ago, but she couldn't think about that now.

For the moment she'd focus on the baby and the festival and her job and kids. That was plenty.

She put on a pot of soup, then brought her laptop to the couch while Jessie slept. When Tee walked in at 2:55, she spotted the baby and almost squealed.

She fought the urge when she realized Jessie was sleeping. "Mom, how cool! This is like the best surprise. Can I hold her when she's awake?" She whispered the words, a rare occurrence where Tee was concerned.

"Sure. If you get your homework done now, it should work out."

"I had a study hall so there isn't much."

"Bonus!"

Tee grinned. She took her backpack to the table and got to work, but every couple of minutes she glanced over and couldn't hold back a smile.

Some kids liked the idea of babies and little kids but couldn't deal with the reality. Not Tee. Her new little cousins could be pesky, cute, whiny or messy and Tee took it in stride. She had the makings of a good babysitter and was getting plenty of practice with Corinne's new nieces and nephews. But every now and then Corinne caught her watching the uncles with their babies. With their toddlers. A look of longing, or maybe *wonder* was a better word, would soften Tee's face.

Was she imagining what it would be like to have a dad? What her life would be like if Dave had lived?

He'd have made sure she got out on the water.

He'd have taken her fishing every week.

He'd have enjoyed her tomboy aspects and cherished her feminine side.

But he wasn't here, and that loss left Corinne to fill the void somehow. She'd make sure things were different next year. But that didn't fix the mistakes she'd already made this year.

Gabe woke at 3:37, befuddled. He stared at the clock, wondering if it was a.m. or p.m., then noted the cloudy but light afternoon.

He jumped up, panicked, and stared at the empty crib.

Jessie.

His heart raced before reality dawned.

Corinne had taken her next door.

He breathed as fear and relief battled within. His pulse pounded. His breath slammed tight against his chest.

His fingers shook. The ends tingled as if on fire.

Shell shock grabbed him in a whole-body press and refused to let go.

He couldn't do this. The thought of something happening to this baby didn't scare him. It drove him positively, absolutely insane. No way could he handle the day-to-day responsibility of a child again. He'd been granted that gift once and lost it of his own accord. He didn't deserve a second chance, despite Adrianna's words to the contrary.

Make some coffee and get hold of yourself.

Then think: life has thrust you into a new situation that pushes old buttons. What would you tell a friend? What advice would you have?

He knew the answer to that.

He'd tell them to get back on the horse that threw them and ride, but they weren't talking theory here. The blessing of a child, a living, breathing human being, should never be taken lightly.

His conscience stayed strangely quiet. Agreeing?

Possibly.

But maybe wishing he would move on, only he couldn't. He shouldn't. And if his head didn't understand that, his heart did.

He made a quick cup of coffee and took a sip before he should have. The pain on the roof of his mouth was nothing compared with the ache in his chest, but he'd dealt with both before. He'd do it again.

He cleaned up in a hurry, then thought twice and shaved. The baby had seemed taken aback by his whiskers, and the last thing he wanted to do was make her cry.

He jogged next door, raised his hand to

knock and paused. Then his heart jump-started again, but for a very different reason.

Corinne was curled against the nearest corner of the couch, feet propped on a pillow, with the baby snuggled against her chest.

Utter contentment.

The beauty of the moment calmed his turmoil but not his pulse.

Corinne had been denied a lot in life. Watching her with the baby made him wish things could have been different for her.

She leaned back slightly, pressed a kiss to Jessie's soft head and glanced up.

Their eyes met.

His heart beat harder. Stronger. The breath he'd just gotten back seemed taken away, but not by fear this time. By something else, an emotion so tender and raw it seemed to swallow him whole.

She waved him in, breaking the moment, and by the time he crossed the floor, he second-guessed himself. It would be foolish to be caught up in the romance of a moment when life held so many turns and twists he wasn't free to take. He crouched down by her side and lifted a brow.

"She likes being cuddled," Corinne whispered, the baby's eyes pinched closed in sleep.

"I see that." He whispered, too. "I think you're both enjoying this."

"Immensely." She had the baseball channel on, with the volume turned down but not off. "Callan, Brandon, Eric and Tee are in the family room getting ready for game seven."

He'd missed game six of the current World Series yesterday, and hadn't even given it a thought.

"Since my Yankees didn't even make the playoffs, I can be indifferent to the outcome."

"No stake in the game, less emotion."

"Exactly. A means to avoid utter disappointment. But a woman must learn to guard her heart, right?"

Her expression indicated she meant more than sports teams. He knew he shouldn't follow that up, but he couldn't help himself, another unusual move. "Except that if we guard against everything, do we block all of our chances at joy?"

"Not with two kids," she whispered, smiling. "They're priority number one, and the years are flying by with them. I kind of hate that."

Her regret painted another picture for him.
Corinne.
A baby.
A child to raise, together.

The thought held an appealing mix of hope for the future.

His palms grew itchy, and he backed off the image instantly. He couldn't trust his brain or his emotional reactions to be normal about kids, and being sleep deprived was obviously not in his best interests.

Until he could—if he ever could—he had no right to tempt fate. "Do you want me to take her?" Part of him wanted her to say no, while another part longed to protect.

"Yes. The soup is all set, but the rolls need to go into the oven."

"Everything smells amazing."

"A cozy fire, homemade soup and a clean baby." She handed him the baby and stood. "A recipe for pure happiness. The simple things in life are the best. And if having Jessie here means you need someone to cover for you at the festival, Gabe, that's fine." She spoke softly as she moved to the kitchen. "Between the troopers and Drew's officers, we'll be covered throughout."

"My mom's coming up for the weekend." He kept his voice quiet, too, as he settled himself into the broad recliner. "I called her last night. She filled me in on some family history and said she'd head this way and watch Jessie. She's nice, Corinne. And she loves babies.

She knew Adrianna was expecting, but everyone there thought that Jessie had been given up for adoption. My phone call was a pretty big surprise."

"I expect it was."

He leaned back, almost loving the feel of the baby on his chest, and scared about how easy it would be to fall into a trap he couldn't afford, the trap of love. He'd been there before and had nothing to show for it, but somehow, holding Jessie in Corinne's cozy room made it feel almost possible, and that might be scarier yet.

Gabe's mother was coming to help, and that meant he'd be at the festival next weekend. She hadn't realized how much she counted on that until she made the offer to let him shrug off the commitment. But it didn't matter because he'd already taken care of things. She liked that about him. Not every sports coach dotted *i*'s and crossed *t*'s. A lot of them left the organizational skills to others.

Not Gabe. He accepted help, but he liked being in charge. So did she. Maybe that's why she wasn't as irked when he'd agreed with the new festival changes against her wishes. He wasn't on the committee to promote himself or a local business like some others. He was there because he truly liked to give back to the community. That meant a great to deal to all of the Gallagher clan, but especially to Corinne. She'd grown up in the midst of dysfunction, so she enjoyed doing whatever she could do to make the community a solid place for families. While that was noble enough, she'd stretched herself too thin, and time with Tee had suffered by her choices. But no more.

She puttered about the kitchen, pretending to be busy, avoiding the inviting picture of Gabe snuggling that baby in her living room. Tonight she'd sit down and make a list of why she needed to downplay her attraction, especially with this new turn of events.

She'd been raising kids on her own for a dozen years. She loved the gift of them, and she'd made a pledge to never put Tee and Callan into a heartbreaking situation. She wasn't foolish enough to think romance developed in a vacuum when a whole family was involved. She knew better. And she'd made cops firmly off-limits years ago.

But this...

She peeked into the living room. Jessie was splayed out against the big guy's chest, sound asleep and perfectly content.

Old dreams resurfaced. Thoughts of the happily-ever-after that had been wrenched away came forth. This was exactly how she'd envisioned her life with Dave, and then suddenly he was gone.

"Mom, is supper almost ready?" Callan's question made for a perfect interruption.

"Yes. Twenty minutes. Can you get out the plates and silverware?"

"Can it wait till a commercial?"

She raised an eyebrow. "Missing sixty seconds of the pregame won't kill you."

"I'll do it." Tee came into the dining area separating the living room from the kitchen of her own accord. "You can watch the pregame, Cal."

He stared at her as if she'd just grown two heads for good reason. Tee might like her brother most of the time, but she championed equal distribution of chores. Volunteering to do double duty wasn't exactly her norm, but Callan was smart enough to grab the offer and run. "Thanks."

Tee set the table carefully. She didn't slide the plates somewhat close to a chair and pile the silverware into the middle like she usually did. Rounding the curve of the oval table, every fork and knife and spoon went into its proper place.

She put matching glasses at each place, just above the spoons, and Corinne wasn't sure if she should comment on the pretty table or call for a medical intervention. She leaned in close as Tee put fresh butter—not the half-used stick on the counter—at each end of the table. "This looks great, Tee. Thank you."

Tee folded napkins—real napkins, not half sheets of paper toweling, which was their norm—beneath each fork. "Everyone should know how to set a table, right?"

Sure they should. And Corinne had been showing them the right way for years, but with the exception of Christmas and Easter, this was the first time one of her kids actually did it. "Yes. They should."

The buzzer for the warmed bread sounded as the boys came up the four steps from the lower-level family room. Brandon whistled in appreciation when he saw the food and the perfect table. "Wow. This looks nice, Mrs. Gallagher."

"Tee did it," Corinne replied before she looked up, but when she raised her gaze, she glimpsed her new reality.

A flush of color brightened Tee's cheeks.

Her normally nonchalant, take-no-prisoners daughter blushed with pleasure over a simple housekeeping task because a boy commented on it. And not just any boy... Callan's friend Brandon.

"Yeah, and I didn't have to do it," Callan

added. He slapped Tee lightly on the back like she was one of the guys. "She's all right. Some of the time," he added. "Hey, did you guys see Coach's baby?"

"Coach has a baby?" Brandon asked.

"Shh. She's sleeping," Tee cautioned.

"She was, but I think the smell of good food has lured her awake." Gabe stood up and raised the baby to his broad shoulder as if he'd been doing it for years.

"Is she yours, Coach?" Brandon's brows shot up as if the image of his coach with a baby didn't add up.

"I'm babysitting her for a while." Gabe handled the boys' curiosity as if he fielded awkward questions on a regular basis. As a cop, he probably did. "And from the scrunched-up look on her face, I think she's going to need a bottle."

Corinne had set one in a small pot of hot water earlier. She tested the temperature on her wrist and reached for the baby. "You come eat. I'll feed her."

"No, I've got it." His hand closed over the bottle. "I can eat when she's done."

"So can I," Corinne argued.

"How about this?" Tee swiped the bottle from her mother's hands and took a seat on the recliner. "I took the babysitting course the town offered last spring, and I want people to hire me for babysitting this year, so I can practice on Jessie. Okay?" She tipped her face up with such a sweet, sincere smile that Corinne had to pause.

"You don't mind, Tee?" Gabe asked. Mixed emotions played across his face. He looked hungry, still tired and a little nervous.

"There's only one way to get practice, Coach. And that's by practicing."

"True words." He handed her the baby, watched while she settled her into a proper position for feeding, and then as she touched the bottle to the baby's soft, pink lips.

Jessie rooted instantly, hands clenched, so happy to be fed, a delightfully normal reaction.

"Coach, do you think we can do batting practice sessions at the dome this week?" Eric asked as he buttered a hunk of warm bread. The dome was a huge, rounded, tent-like facility where kids could sharpen their athletic skills indoors during the winter.

Gabe shook his head. "Not until January, guys. I've got to juggle babysitting, work, the festival and help cover a couple of guys who are taking vacation in December. Once January hits, we'll book time there, twice a week. Same as always."

"And the weather's been unusually mild,"

Corinne noted. "Can't you guys do batting practice right here at Welch Grove Park?"

"It gets dark early now." Callan shrugged. "By the time we get home from school and get to the park it's already dusk."

"The shortened days make a difference," Gabe agreed. He paused as he ladled soup into his bowl, then breathed deep and faced Corinne. "I don't think I've ever smelled anything so good, Corinne." He smiled her way, the ladle paused midair.

Pleasure warmed her cheeks, much the way her daughter's had a few minutes before. "Thank you."

"You're welcome."

Behind them, the baby gasped like they often do when they need to burp after a milky feast.

Gabe shot out of his chair. "I'll take her, Tee."

Tee wasn't exactly the acquiescent type. "Coach, I've got her. She's fine." She stood up and walked the baby around the room, patting her back like an expert. "I had to do this with Davy last year. And Emily's baby, too. Practice, remember?"

Gabe's hands clenched. His face went tight.

"Hey, you're actually pretty good with a kid, Tee." Brandon offered the praise around a bite of bread, total boy. "I wouldn't have a clue what to do with a baby, and I sure wouldn't touch it. I think they're breakable. They've got to be. They're so small."

"Mom says they're tougher than they look," Tee offered over her shoulder.

"I'll take her, Tee. Go grab some food." Gabe's voice didn't leave room for argument. He reached out and took Jessie into his arms, then picked up the bottle to continue feeding her.

An awkward silence descended.

Tee's expression spoke plainly. Gabe was making a big deal out of nothing, but Corinne was grateful when she held her tongue. She came to the table and took the remaining seat, facing Brandon, then proceeded to look anywhere but at him.

Smitten.

The boys talked sports, ranging from current football to the last baseball game of the year, being played that night. Instead of wolfing her food, Tee ate in tiny bites, eyes down. She didn't join in the conversation and the boys didn't appear to notice, too busy dissecting team moves and managers and unanimously deciding that Mike Trout was the best player in baseball.

And Gabe sat straight and still, not leaning

against the recliner's cushioned back, as if he didn't dare allow himself to be comfortable with the baby in his arms but couldn't let her go, either.

Seeing that, Corinne couldn't help but wonder why.

Corinne thought babies were tougher than they looked.

She was wrong, and Gabe understood that better than most. Kids were delicate creatures in so many ways. Gifts from God, deserving of love and attention and protection.

Aware of Corinne's gaze, he kept his eyes trained on Jessie. She squirmed, then did that gasping thing again as she tried to pull back from the bottle.

Gracie had never done that, she'd never made that strangling sound that made him leap out of his chair a few moments before. Jessie appeared to think it was quite normal, but that was because she didn't know how his heart rose up in his chest, strangling him from within. She scrunched up her little face, writhed as if in dire pain, burped and smiled.

And not just any smile.

She pulled back from his chest with her head still a little wobbly, and that precious baby met him eye-to-eye and grinned as if happy to be fed and proud to have burped.

He grinned back.

He didn't want to, but he couldn't help it. The response was automatic, and when she read his smile, hers grew.

She reached out to touch his face like she'd done the previous day, and this time she didn't frown.

"She's glad you shaved," Corinne observed. She moved to his side and rubbed her head against the baby's onesie-covered belly.

Jessie laughed, grabbed for Corinne's hair and missed because Corinne drew back.

"I've got her." Corinne reached for the baby. "Go eat, and don't give me a hard time, Coach. House rules."

"Did you get enough?" He glanced at the table and was amazed by how much food three teenage boys had plowed through. "Never mind. If I don't eat now, I'll miss my chance."

"Growing boys." Corinne settled the baby onto the floor and changed her diaper while he returned to the table. "Cal, since Tee set the table, can you and the guys load the dishwasher?"

"Sure," Eric answered as he stood. "That was great, Mrs. G. Thanks for letting us stay and watch the first half of the game with you guys tonight."

"It's a school night, but when it's the World Series, exceptions must be made," she told him. "And we're happy to have you guys over." She finished changing the baby, then set up a play mat with overhanging arches. "I'm glad I kept this tucked away when Emily's baby got too big for it. Gabe, look." She tucked the baby onto the mat, face up. Jessie began reaching and kicking immediately, batting at the soft-sided toys suspended above. "She loves this."

She did, and that spawned another memory. He and Elise, watching Grace's growth, noting every one of her newly acquired skills in a baby book. Rolling over, first smile, first tooth, first tear…

His heart tripped again.

There was no way he could do this, not when every time he looked at Jessie, all he could see was Grace at the same age. He wasn't sure his head could handle it, and he knew his heart couldn't, but what could he do?

No answers came, and maybe that was because God wanted him to make up his own mind.

He knew what he'd tell someone else. He'd done it often enough. He'd tell them to move forward, grasp the good of today and forge on.

That was easy advice to give away, but wretchedly hard to follow himself.

"Stop fretting over whatever and eat," Corinne scolded from the floor. "Take it day by day, the same kind of thing you'd tell the team, I expect."

She was right. He didn't think he could eat a bite, then proceeded to wolf down a monster-sized bowl of soup and two thick slices of her homemade bread, drizzled with garlic butter. When he finally pushed back from the table, he stared down, dumbfounded. "I can't believe I ate all that."

"You have to remember to take care of yourself in order to take care of her," she reminded him softly. The baby started fussing, and Corinne turned her over on her tummy and rubbed her back. A little burp followed, then a sigh of contentment when she took her pacifier and dozed off. Eat and sleep, with occasional diaper changes.

The normal routine came roaring back to him, the beloved sameness of it all amid the wonder of new life.

"Come sit or stretch out. And if you doze off, I'll watch her for you. I'll stay right here," Corinne promised. She stood and crossed the room to retrieve her laptop, then settled onto the floor alongside the sofa. "That recliner is mighty comfy, and if she stays awake tonight, a little extra rest now isn't a bad idea."

He was 100 percent sure he wouldn't fall

asleep, so when he awakened during the fourth inning, he was surprised. The baby was still sleeping, Tee was watching the game and Corinne was stretching tired joints. "Hey. Look who's awake," she teased softly, smiling. "Mr. I'm-Sure-I-Won't-Fall-Asleep has rejoined us."

"I crashed." He pushed the recliner more upright and yawned. "I thought I was tougher than that."

"Food, cozy fire and sleeping baby." Corinne set the laptop aside and stood. "Perfect combination. Coffee?"

"I'll get it. You've been working."

"Well, I'm done working, and I'm having tea, so I'm heading that way." She popped a refillable pod into the coffee dispenser and hit the button just as Jessie began to squeak. "And it looks like we've got company."

He bent low to pick up the baby. She blinked round eyes at him, yawned, stretched and blinked again. "I'll do the diaper if you do coffee."

"Deal." She brought two mugs to the living room almost instantly and Gabe realized how much he loved the new single-cup brewing system when she set the coffee on the table to his left. "I've got her bottle ready whenever she is."

"How are you so good at this when it's been twelve years?" he asked with a nod toward Tee.

She ticked off her fingers. "Kimberly and Drew's little guy, Davy; Emily's baby, Katelyn; not to mention the twins, Timmy and Dolly. And I work with expectant parents. Lots of times I dash across the floor to meet their tiny blessings when they come."

She went above and beyond. He'd noticed that quality in her right off, but he'd noticed something else, too. Corinne kept an intentional cool distance around him. At least she had until he found a bundle of joy on his doorstep. Funny how a baby changed all kinds of boundaries when you least expected it.

He walked Jessie around the room. Tee glanced up, then down.

He'd hurt her feelings.

What an oaf.

He sat on the edge of the window seat and pointed to the homework pile next to her. "Social studies?"

"A geographical map of the New England colonies with at least ten topographical features."

It looked pretty good from where he was sitting. "If you're ready for a break, would you like to feed her so I can talk to your mom about the Christkindl festival next week?"

Her eyes lit up, but Tee feared nothing, a fact

he liked. "Are you going to get all nervous and overreact if she makes a noise?"

Corinne kept her eyes down across the room, but he was pretty sure she choked back a laugh.

"No, and I'm sorry I did. You were doing fine. Blame it on my inexperience and nerves, okay?"

She met his gaze and drew her forehead tight. "Coach, I've never seen you get nervous like that before. Even in the championships. Not like..." She shrugged, thinking. "Ever."

"Babies are way more important than any game," he answered softly, and when he did, he read acceptance in her gaze.

"My mom would say the same thing." She flipped her notebook closed, set it on top of the poster board and stood. "I'd love to feed Jessie."

"Here you go." He handed her the baby, then brought her the bottle and a cotton towel for burping. "You feed. I'll work."

"Gotcha."

And when Jessie gurgled that weird sound a few minutes later, he steeled himself not to turn, look or jump out of his skin. Tee handled her just fine. Now if he could only learn to do the same.

Chapter Nine

Gabe's living room lights were dimmed but still glowing late that evening. Should she offer to help? Or leave him to his struggles?

Corinne's hand hesitated over the light switch, and then she flicked it off, darkening the first floor. He'd be fine. He seemed to almost have an affinity for baby care, unusual for someone with no experience, but his fear was real and she'd seen that often at the hospital. It would dissipate in a few days, and by then he'd have child care lined up from the list she'd given him, and a few days with his mother around. That week of organization and help should bolster his confidence.

By Thursday night, when vendors had rolled into town and the huge tents had been erected on the Shelby/Gallagher Farm, she was ready to head home when Susie MacIntosh hailed her from the shuttle bus drop-off loop. She crossed her way quickly. "How are you doing? I keep thinking about you and this baby." Corinne kept her voice soft on purpose.

"Good so far," Susie whispered back. "Mack is so excited, and we've never gotten past three months before, so there's reason to be optimistic, right? We're almost halfway there!"

"Yes, absolutely." Corinne gave her a quick hug. "Infertility is a wretched business, Susie, and I'm praying for you guys and this baby. Every single day. Are you helping with the festival?"

Susie shook her head. "No, but Mack is, and I decided to check things out as the vendors put things in place."

"Wasn't Gabe on tonight's schedule?" Corinne asked. Susie's quick expression of regret was enough of an answer. "Did he take the night off because of the baby?"

"He took the whole week off," said Mack as he came up alongside. "He's nervous about day care. And maybe still wondering what to do."

"I assumed he'd found someone and went to work like usual." The past few days had been a whirlwind of work and festival organization. She hadn't noticed that Gabe wasn't leaving the house. "Mack, thank you for jumping in to help. It's greatly appreciated. Are you covering his schedule for tomorrow, too?"

"He's done the same for me many times." He looped an arm around his wife and shared a sad kind of smile with her. "His mom rolls in tonight, so he's fine for the weekend. But he needs to figure this out. If you have any influence, Corinne…"

He said the words as if he thought she did, and the minute he said it, she wished it were true. She moved toward her car and hit the key fob to disengage the locks. "I don't, but I'm bossy. We'll see. Thanks again for stepping in tonight."

They waved goodbye and headed in the opposite direction while she navigated trucks and trailers to get out onto the road.

Gabe hadn't worked all week.

She needed to smack him.

She pulled into her driveway, dead tired from the craziness of festival prep, but headed across the yard first. If she went inside her cozy home, she'd never have the energy to come back out and scold her tall, good-looking, stubborn neighbor. She rapped on his door lightly.

He opened it a few seconds later, looking surprised. "Hey. Come on in, it's getting cold out there."

"The weather's ready to turn, for sure," she answered as he swung the door shut behind her. "Mack ratted you out tonight."

He frowned.

"He said you took this week off and that you're not sure what to do about day care for Jessie, which means you didn't go visit any of the places I gave you."

"I did go, actually." He looked uncomfortable and swiped a hand to the nape of his neck. "I didn't like them, Corinne. They seemed so…" He hesitated, then said, "Sterile. Like it was a schoolhouse setting for infants. And who wants that for a baby?"

She didn't tell him that lots of people preferred the more professional setting, because it was clear that he wasn't a fan. "So you're just going to stay home for the next five years until she's in kindergarten?"

He grimaced. She took pity on him because he seemed truly uncomfortable about leaving the baby in a structured day care facility. "Kate is free right now, and she offered to watch her, but I thought we had this all set. She managed to raise a bunch of Gallaghers, so why don't you think about that. If nothing else, it buys you some time."

"You think she'd do it?" Gabe's expression

was like a drowning man, grabbing for a newly extended lifeline. "Seriously?"

"She said she would, and when Drew needed a place for Jessie to stay overnight, Kate jumped all over the opportunity," she reminded him. "Kimberly has the event center running smoothly, and Kate likes that she can actually be retired unless needed. So yes, she'd love it."

"I would be okay with that," he told her, and the relief on his face agreed. "I've got their number, I just didn't want to impose. I'll call her."

"Good. And even if having Jess is temporary, at least you can both get into some kind of normal routine. I know you've been up late and up early because I see the lights, but one lesson that every new parent learns is that they have to try to work in some sort of normal. Otherwise they drive themselves crazy trying to be all things to all people. Especially babies. Like the one peeking up at me over there."

She crossed the room.

The minute Jess spotted her, she grinned and batted little arms, wanting to be lifted and held. "Oh, you absolutely marvelous, adorable thing." Corinne scooped her up and laughed into her happy baby face. "You are beyond precious, my darling. And have you been keeping my friend up night and day?" When the baby laughed, Corinne nuzzled her cheek, then scolded. "Shame on you, but I do understand the attraction."

Did she just say that out loud?

Heat rose from somewhere in her middle, a reaction she couldn't let him see. Eyes down, she kept her attention firmly on the baby.

"You understand the attraction, Corinne?" He'd moved closer, and the deep note of his voice commanded the tiny hairs along her neck to attention. He sounded...interested. The very thing she'd been trying to guard against.

"We girls are always attracted to anyone who brings us food," she offered lightly, as if his proximity wasn't tempting her forward. "And this happy smile says you're doing something right. She's absolutely content."

"She is. I'm growing attached." Gabe frowned and rubbed his neck again, then geared his attention toward the baby. "I probably shouldn't, right?"

"Oh, Gabe. You'd be wrong not to, but I can't speak to that. I know there are a lot of variables to consider."

Twin headlights flashed in the driveway. A car pulled up, shut off the engine, and then a lithe woman crossed the concrete walk. "Mom's here."

He crossed the room and opened the door.

His mother blew in like a category three hurricane, laughing and hugging him, scolding and then hugging him again before she spotted Corinne. "Oh, well, well, well! Gabe Cutler, who is this lovely woman holding this equally lovely baby? And this baby looks just like Adrianna, doesn't she?"

Gabe sent an incredulous look from her to Jessie and back. "You can't possibly expect me to know this. I was a kid, and I sure wasn't paying attention to babies."

"Good point." His mother crossed the room and extended a hand. "I'm Linda Cutler. It is so nice to meet you. Whoever you are."

Funny, warm and a little cryptic. Corinne liked her on the spot. She hooked her thumb toward the north and said, "Next-door neighbor and festival committee member. And I help with the baseball team during the season."

"And she's great with babies," Gabe added. "And makes the best soup I've had in a long while."

"Hmm?" Linda's eyes lit with interest. "All things that are good to know. May I take her?" She reached for Jessie and Corinne handed her over.

"Of course. I'm heading out, and Gabe, call Kate," she reminded him. "Watching Jess will give her so much pleasure, and she'll show her off all over town."

"A Gallagher trait."

"Yes." She smiled because he was right, and she was okay with that. "The town will fall in love with their new resident, and that's never a bad thing. Mrs. Cutler." She extended her hand toward Gabe's mother. "So nice to meet you. And you." She faced Gabe as she crossed to the side door. "I'll see you at the festival tomorrow, okay?"

"I'll be there. Corinne?"

She'd been heading out but paused and looked back.

"Thanks for checking up on me."

His mother hummed again, a soft sound of approval that they both ignored. "That's what neighbors are for, right?"

"Right."

His smile deepened, but she was pretty sure that was pure relief. His mother had come for the weekend, Kate would jump at the chance to help out with the baby while Gabe sorted things out, and the combination had just lifted stress off his shoulders. Reason enough to smile, right there. She wrote it off as that, when he followed her out the door. "I'll see you home."

"It's a hundred feet, Gabe."

"It's dark and cold and I wanted to thank you in private." He glanced toward his house and the silhouette of his mother, walking the baby inside. "I appreciate it, Corinne. More than you know."

"Gabe." She shivered and made a face at him. "It's getting colder out here and you've already thanked me. Go visit with your mother."

She gazed up at him, letting her smile soften the words, and when he gazed down...when his attention drifted to her lips as if wondering... her heart sped up.

She wondered, too. She'd been wondering for what seemed like a long while, and it was ridiculous because she knew better. She'd set limits purposely, for good reason.

He settled his hands on her shoulders, and his touch was enough to warm her one way and inspire shivers in a very different manner.

He leaned in slightly.

So did she.

Cool fresh air puffed the scent of baby powder and coffee around her.

Then her cell phone signaled a call from her house phone. Tee, wondering what was keeping her so long.

She took a step back.

Tee thought the world of Gabe. Callan did, too. So how weird would it get if the responsible adults began a relationship that didn't work out?

Gabe was Callan's coach, and now their neighbor. A bad move for either of them could have disastrous effects, with way too much fallout. How could they risk roughing up their current dynamics?

They couldn't. Callan's baseball talent could take him places she'd never dreamed of. College scouts had already told the local varsity coach that they were watching three local players develop, and that Callan Gallagher topped their lists.

And Tee thought the world of Gabe.

No, romance gone bad messed things up, and even if he wasn't a state trooper, she had to put kids first.

Or you could admit that you're scared. That burying your husband rocked you to the core and you're afraid to take chances again.

Corinne ignored the mental scolding as she hurried back to the warmth of her living room. There was nothing wrong with being protective. With putting others first. With watching out for her children.

Did that mean she limited her options?

Yes, by choice.

But when she turned off the kitchen light

a little later, lamplight spilled across Gabe's side yard.

The Penski house had been dark for a long time, and while the new occupant managed to jumble her nerves, the sight of that slanted glow seemed nice. She'd have to learn to be his neighbor. Just his neighbor. But she couldn't deny liking that she had a big, broad-shouldered cop living right next door.

Gabe had volunteered his time with the Christkindl for the past three years because it was the right thing to do. A fundraiser that helped the families of fallen first responders meant a lot. But he'd always taken road duty before. His presence kept folks safe as they crossed the busy road leading into town, and the sight of his light-flashing cruiser kept speeds down on the main road. His assignment offered enough degrees of separation to keep him focused on the normal, everyday busyness of traffic control and leave the holiday hoopla to others.

Not this year. He'd been home all week and the commander had put him on festival detail, right at the sprawling tent site on the vintage Gallagher farm.

He exited his car only to be immediately engulfed in all things Christmas.

Twinkle lights surrounded him.

A surround-sound speaker system played upbeat carols.

Decorations lined booth after booth, pretty and poignant.

The man who avoided Christmas found himself immersed. Five minutes in and he wanted to make a mad dash to the road, grab a comrade and change assignments.

Are you going to make the holidays dark and silent for that baby? How is that the right thing to do? his inner voice mocked him softly.

He kept to the outside of the tents as much as he could, but that didn't negate the music and the merry lights, or festooned fresh wreaths in an open-air nursery set up just inside the festival entrance.

"Gabe."

Corinne's voice called to him. He turned quickly because this close to the festival entrance, he might still be able to make a run for it.

He paused in his tracks and couldn't hold back a grin when he spotted her over-the-top holiday outfit.

"I'm rockin' the Ugliest Christmas Sweater, right?" She turned, laughing, and he had to scrub his hand to his jaw to control his response.

"You've entered the festival contest, I take it."

She beamed. "I could win with this, don't you think?"

Oh, he thought all right. He thought she was the cutest, sassiest woman he'd met in a long time. He thought she rocked that sweater, because while the ornamentation on the sweater was boldly Christmas-themed to the point of disbelief, the figure inside was total woman. "They could not have fit another clichéd holiday image on that thing."

She nodded, smug, and looped her arm through his. "Exactly why I grabbed it at the thrift store for three whole dollars." She leaned closer, smelling of some kind of holiday cheer. Cookies and fruit, maybe? He wasn't sure, but he longed to lean closer. "I'm steering you this way before you make a run for it, because you appeared to be looking for an escape hatch when I spotted you."

He couldn't deny it. Not with her, and that surprised him. "I was, actually."

She didn't push. She simply squeezed his arm lightly as she pointed out all the different vendors, and the massive heaters blowing warm air into the house-sized canvas tents. "With the festival site over a mile from town, we always provide a police escort to vendors who do money drops at noon and three. If you or one of the other officers can escort them to their cars, they can go to the Grace Haven banks and make deposits."

"Don't most of them use debit cards?"

She lifted one pretty shoulder, and the sweet scent assailed him again. "A lot of folks do, but there're a few who use cash. Of course, with the shuttle buses to town, sales here might take a downturn." She swept the crowded tent with a pensive look. "We'll see."

"Have you had to take it on the chin from the vendors?" he asked softly. She shook her head, but he read more in her expression. "From some, I take it."

"That's accurate enough," she admitted. "I'm hoping their concerns are overdone and that they go home happy after a successful sale. Which means they'll come back next year."

"And will you chair it again?" He kept the low tone purposely because she didn't need others overhearing her concerns.

She shook her head. "It's time to move on. Not so much because of the changes, but because I've put in my time. In a few years the kids will be off to college." She made a face of regret. "It's gone so fast, and I can't believe that part of my life is close to being over. That was never the plan, but plans change, it seems."

He knew that as well as she did, but she

handled it better. So much better. Probably because she was an innocent victim while he carried a yoke of guilt.

"How's your mom doing with Jess?" she asked as they moved toward the food tent. Delicious scents filled the air. Simmering apple, sweet cinnamon and some kind of fried-dough decadence mingled with German strudels baking in an oven adapted for outdoor use.

"She's great," he admitted. "And she filled me in on some things that need consideration. Have you got time to talk later?" He faced her fully. "Like at the end of the day? Or tomorrow?" The shuttles were scheduled to pick up the first festivalgoers at the high school now, which meant the time for conversation would be over once the first bus rolled through the loop. "This whole thing with my aunt and uncle has me confused. I know what I want to do, but I'm not sure it's the right thing."

"Tonight is good because the kids are staying at Kate and Pete's house this weekend. They both had things on their schedules, so it was easier on everyone if they stay in town with Grandma and Grandpa."

"Then how about if we hit the Thruway Café about six o'clock? Is that good?"

A voice called her name. Then another, from the opposite side of the long tented aisle. She fluttered a hand as she moved to the first vendor. "I'll meet you there."

He moved toward a less holiday-themed side of the tent. He passed jams and jellies and candles and jewelry booths, but came to a complete stop when he spotted baby clothes.

He swallowed hard but couldn't resist running his finger along the soft, nubbed bright red fabric hanging at the booth's edge.

"So beautiful, right?" An older woman smiled at him as she entered the booth with a steaming cup of hot chocolate. She set the mug down on the back table, far from the handmade goods, then moved forward. "My daughter does the baby clothes and blankets. And she can embroider names on them, see?" She held up a blanket and he saw the name "Annie" embroidered around the satin binding. "We can customize most anything, but of course, a beautiful dress like this one." She pointed to the one he'd paused to admire. "Needs nothing else. It says Christmas without being ostentatious."

That's what drew him to the red-and-white dress. It was tastefully simple and not overdone with holiday adornment. "How big is it? I mean what size is it?" he corrected himself, flustered. He hadn't bought a little girl outfit in a long, long time.

"This one is six months. How old is your baby?"

His heart scrunched because Jess wasn't his for real. But she was his for now, and so he lifted his shoulders. "Jess is four and a half months old, and she's not real big for her age, according to my mother."

"With Christmas next month, I think this size would work. And being a dress, you don't have to worry about length so much. Not with the pretty little stockings." The vendor had attached a pair of white stockings to the hanger, and the feet of the stockings looked like an old-school pair of black patent leather shoes. Like the ones Grace used to wear. She'd pretend they were tap shoes and dance around the house, tapping her toes with or without music.

He pulled his hand back.

And then the rest of his body followed.

His radio came alive and he eased away from the booth as if he was needed someplace else. He wasn't, it was a general check-in call from the road, but the thought of buying that dress pushed his heart into overdrive.

He went through the morning pretending he had blinders on. He ignored the fuss and fun, he kept his eyes on people, not things, and by midafternoon he was congratulating himself that he'd almost made it when an old-fashioned Kris Kringle strolled through the tent crowds, handing out peppermint sticks to the shoppers.

As Gabe lingered along the back row, keeping a quiet eye on things, a shopper lifted the red dress from the crochet vendor's display.

A part of him hoped she'd buy the tiny dress and take it out of temptation's reach.

Another part wanted to cut across the floor and snatch it out of her hands, and when she flipped the price tag over, scanned it and set the dress down with regret, relief swept him.

He was being ridiculous. Jess needed clothes, he was her guardian at least for the time being, and the outfit was charming.

But what if his aunt and uncle fought for custody once they discovered he had this baby?

Should he fight to keep her? Was he being too judgmental? Or was it important for someone to finally recognize Adrianna's right as a mother to help form her child's future?

He moved away from the pretty dress and the older woman's understanding gaze and made himself a deal. If the dress was still there near closing time on Saturday, he'd buy it. If not…then it wasn't meant to be.

Chapter Ten

Coffee with Gabe.

Not a date, not a date, not a date...

Corinne muttered the phrase repeatedly as she headed for the café not far from the Thruway exit. The café in town was lovely, and she loved the Grace Haven diner, but both would be mobbed with people they knew. This one was just far enough outside town to draw travelers, not locals. Here they could sit and talk in relative peace without becoming gossip fodder. She parked the car and spotted Gabe, waiting outside.

Chivalrous.

He could have escaped the brisk wind and the growing chill by grabbing a table for them, but he didn't. He'd waited in the cold for her, and that made everything so much nicer. "Hey."

He reached out a hand for hers as naturally

as if he did it every day, and that made her wish he did. "They're calling for snow by mid-week. And not a few flakes, either. The real thing."

His hand clasped hers in a move so smooth she wasn't sure where his skin began and hers ended. "Thanks for meeting me."

"Glad to do it," she told him, looking up.

Big mistake.

The minute her gaze met his, all she could think of was that near kiss on the deck, and wonder what she was missing by not kissing Gabe.

She dropped her gaze and spotted an empty corner table as they moved indoors. "How about that one? Quiet enough to be private, open enough to enjoy the carols."

"As if we didn't have enough of those today."

She settled into her side of the booth and frowned. "I love Christmas music. I love the sweet ones, the romantic ones, the funny ones. I love hymns and carols, and I will admit to playing Christmas music throughout the year as the spirit moves me. Does that make me crazy?"

"The fact that you asked the question should be enough of an answer," he teased, but she wasn't immune to the sorrow in his manner.

"The pain of Christmas." She said the words

softly and covered his hand with hers. "When things go well, the holidays are such a joy. But in despair or sorrow, they become a sharp-edged sword. I've seen many a grief-stricken family through those first holidays after a loss, and it's heartbreaking, Gabe."

"I bet it is."

His simple words agreed, but she'd read the anguish in his face over the past week. The holidays had a way of magnifying loss. She understood that from a personal and profes-sional perspective. But Gabe's angst had fired up the moment he'd found that baby at his door and hadn't dissipated yet.

"Are you hungry, Corinne?"

She shook her head. "I stopped by the stru-del booth twice today. Hannah Guerst's home-made strudels are my guilty pleasure. Her shop is far enough away that I don't get them often, but during festival time I eat as much as I want. My reward for a year of work well done."

"Do you have a favorite?"

"Too many," she admitted, but the question made her smile. "Anything with cinnamon. I love the apple varieties, but I think the brown sugar pecan with maple glaze is my favorite."

"Anything with brown sugar, maple and nuts should be a favorite," he agreed. He stood to place their order with the barista. "Do you want a regular coffee? Or something fancier?"

"Tea," she replied and tapped her slim gold watch. "I've got to be up early and back to the festival grounds, so no coffee tonight. A hot raspberry peach tea sounds marvelous."

He crossed to the barista station and when he came back, he set her tea down first, then sipped his coffee before settling into the booth again. "This is amazingly good coffee. That would be my suggestion to the festival committee for next year. Get someone on-site that can make a decent cup of coffee."

She didn't disagree. "You're right, and that's part of the reason I need to step down. I can't hurt old Milt's feelings by refusing him a spot. He's such a sweet old guy. But his coffee has taken a nosedive, and that's a problem that needs to be solved by someone else. And while I can make small talk as well as anyone, I don't think we came here to talk about coffee, did we?"

"No." He gripped his cup and faced her. "I've filled you in on my cousin and how her parents reacted to her choices and her pregnancy. At this point, they think she gave Jess up for adoption when she was born over four months ago."

Corinne cringed slightly. "Ouch."

"I know." He sipped his coffee with deliberation, then said, "I'm procrastinating purposely, for a mix of reasons, but I'm not sure how to move forward. My fear is that once they know, they'll plead for custody."

"Most grandparents would," she acknowledged. She really couldn't imagine many grandparents who wouldn't.

"That's just it." He leaned forward, hands clasped as he continued in a serious tone. "They're unforgiving people. Their brand of religion doesn't allow for mistakes. They get harsh. And I'm not saying that to excuse what Adrianna's done over the years, but it was almost as if nothing she did would ever please them. So maybe she simply gave up." He studied his mug with grave intent. A muscle in his lower right cheek twitched slightly. "They didn't want damaged goods in a child. They threw Adrianna out. I can't imagine turning Jessie over to them and witnessing the same thing happening again. How unfair would that be to an innocent baby, to knowingly place her into that kind of a situation? And if Adrianna had wanted her parents to have the baby, she'd have arranged it that way. She didn't. That's the stumbling block, because she specifically asked for her parents to be denied custody in her papers."

She lifted her eyebrows, inviting him to continue.

"I'm not perfect, either," he said softly. "I've made mistakes in life, and the thought of raising a baby scares me. But the thought of going against Adrianna's wishes and letting my aunt and uncle take Jess just doesn't sit right. And once they realize where she is, I think they'll fight for her. Or find some way within the family to try to make her life miserable. And I'm not sure I'm strong enough for that."

"For a fight? You?" She sat back, amazed. "Gabe Cutler, I've never met a stronger or fairer man in my life. Of course you're up for it. You rise to any occasion. It's part of who you are. Why is this different? Are you hesitating for the financial reasons of hiring a lawyer? I don't have much, but I'll help if I can."

His smile was part grimace. "Thank you. I love your generous spirit, but, no. It's not money. It's me, Corinne."

"You?" She watched him, puzzled, then sighed. "The past likes to step on the heels of the present, doesn't it? It's so hard to walk fully forward when regret tugs us backward. Do you want to tell me about it? If you do, that's fine. And if not, that's fine, too, Gabe. Either way,

I'm giving you the top slot on my prayer list because I don't like to see you hurting. And I expect," she added softly, leaning forward so no one would hear, "that you've been hurting for a while."

He'd been hurting for more than a while. The ache in his heart had been raw for a very long time. Corinne's sympathy helped, maybe because she sympathized without knowing a thing. He took a deep breath and began. "I was married years ago."

Her open look invited him to continue.

"We had a daughter. Grace." He loosed his hands and gripped the coffee cup hard. "She would have been Tee's age. And she was like Tee in so many ways. Funny. Laughing. Always talking, spontaneous, bright. She was a ray of sunshine that just never seemed to draw a cloud. Beautiful and dear and amazing." His eyes grew wet.

He didn't care.

Because talking about Grace was worth risking his tough-guy image.

"We went to a party, a football party at a friend's house. A bunch of kids, moms and dads. A perfect day. My buddy had put a man cave in his barn. Just a spot where he could watch the games and eat pizza and wings and be loud on game days." He lifted his coffee, changed his mind and set it down again. "Somehow I must have left the door to the car open. It was a beautiful day, the first game of the season, and I disappeared while the women and kids hung out in the backyard and the upstairs family room. It was all so perfect..." He breathed deeply. "Until I heard the scream."

Her hand touched his gently. So gently.

"Somehow Grace had gotten into the car and shut the door. I was the last one out of the car, I was the last one to go into the party, and I must not have shut it right. I was carrying a small cooler of food and shoved it shut with my knee. I thought it closed." He sighed, then shook his head. "It didn't. My wife found Grace in the car, in the hot sun. She thought Grace was playing with the other kids. I was inside, oblivious to my beautiful daughter. And just like that, she was gone."

"Oh, Gabe."

Did she know that tears were streaming down her cheeks? Maybe not, because she did nothing to blot them.

She covered his wrists with her hands. "I am so, so sorry. I can't even imagine your loss."

He pulled one hand free and slid a stack of napkins her way. "I didn't mean to upset you, Corinne. I'm sorry."

"Don't say that. Don't ever say that," she scolded as the warm Christmas hymn about a holy night wove poignant notes in the background. "Sharing hopes and fears and sadness is important. But I'm brokenhearted for you, Gabe. What a weight to carry around for so long." Her expression deepened. She kept her hand on his wrist and squeezed lightly. "No wonder Jessie scares you to death."

"She does," he admitted. "But I'm just as worried about letting her go to her grandparents, because then I'm breaking another sacred trust. And I can't do that, Corinne. I've done it once already, so which fear do I face? The fear of making another grave mistake with an innocent child or the fear of letting others hurt her emotionally for the rest of her life?"

"You didn't ask to be her guardian," she reminded him. "But I can understand your cousin's decision. She looked for someone fair, wise and strong to take care of her baby. She wasn't looking back, Gabe. Adrianna was looking forward. And I think that's what you need to do, too."

Forward.

He'd moved forward physically because he had no choice, but emotionally he'd stayed mired in personal tragedy for years. "There's more, Corinne."

She frowned in sympathy.

"My wife died the next year. We weren't able to get over our loss, and she slipped into a cycle of drinking the pain away. She left me on the one-year anniversary of losing Grace and died in a one-car crash three months later while under the influence of alcohol. And nothing's been quite right since."

She stood, came around the table and slipped in beside him.

And then she hugged him.

She wrapped her arms around him and held him close.

He felt treasured.

He felt undone, unwound, as if part of that tight knot coiled within him had worked itself loose. He cherished the embrace, and the woman offering it. Her solace blessed him, and the scent of her hair mingled with brewing coffee and baking gingerbread. Too soon she released him and leaned back. "You should keep Jessie."

"And shrug off her family?"

"You're her family now. You're the one chosen by the distraught mother. There were reasons she sent her daughter to your protection in her hour of need. Her actions show intent and follow-through. She made her decision known and legalized it as best she could. I can see this is a hard step forward for you. You don't trust yourself."

The accuracy of her words made him swallow hard.

"But you *should* trust yourself, because you've got every quality a child would want in a parent."

Except the one that mattered nine years ago. Protection.

"And I cannot pretend to imagine your pain at losing Grace, but I wish one of those grown-ups who were outside had been paying more attention, too. And I expect there were several who feel just as guilty as you do."

Her words took him by surprise.

He'd heard them before, sure, but this was the first time they'd really registered. Maybe because he hadn't talked about losing Grace and Elise for long, long years. "I can't blame others for my carelessness, Corinne. It would be wrong."

"It would," she whispered back with a gaze so soft and caring that his heart yearned to know hers. To see the world through Corinne's pragmatic optimism for the rest of his life. "It's not about blaming others, Gabe. It never is. It's about forgiving ourselves, and I think Adrianna has given you the best chance to do exactly that. She's offered to let you make decisions for her child during a season of loving and forgiving. The best season of all. Now it's up to you to grab hold and hop on the roller coaster of being a single parent."

She thought he could do this and believed it was in Jessie's best interests.

His phone buzzed a text from his mother. He pulled it out, saw the photo and held it up for Corinne to see.

Baby Jessie, curled up in the soft-sided crib, sound asleep with a hinted smile, and the caption below read Smiling and dreaming of great things to come.

His heart stretched wider, opening the door of possibilities. "I hate that my choice might hurt my aunt and uncle, but my conscience won't let me give Jessie up to them." He took in a deep breath. "I'll let them know I have her, and that I'm her legal guardian. Then we'll take it from there."

"And I'll be right next door, helping all I can," she promised. "We single parents have to stick together."

He turned to smile at her.

She was close.

So close that he could lean just a tiny bit closer and whisper a kiss to that beautiful mouth. And as he contemplated that, he realized he didn't want just a sweet little kiss of friendship.

He wanted to let her know that she wasn't just a neighbor and a friend. She was beyond special and every part of his being wanted her to realize that. He dropped his gaze to her lips again. "Corinne…"

She came closer, so close he felt the warmth of her breath flutter the hairs along his temple.

And then she stopped. She drew back.

Regret shadowed her face. She bit her lip lightly, pensive. "I made a promise to myself, too. When Dave died, and I went through that pain of loss firsthand, I promised myself I would never get involved with another lawman. How could I knowingly put Callan and Tee through that if something were to happen? So as much as I'd love to pursue this—" she indicated his mouth "—I can't, Gabe. I don't think I have it in me to take that risk again."

"But you're tempted? A little?" He raised one brow slightly while he waited, watching her eyes widen in sweet reaction. And then he waited some more.

She was tempted more than a little, and the look on Gabe's face suggested he suspected as much. He'd shared his heart and his pain with her. He'd bared his soul.

More than ever, she longed to care for him. Comfort him.

But her pledge had never been about her. She was tough, faithful and independent enough to trust God's goodness. But to knowingly thrust her children into that situation would be wrong. "Lots of things are tempting, Gabe. But single parents have to weigh a lot more than attraction. I've got three hearts to protect under my roof."

He acknowledged that with a look of acceptance. Then he leaned closer, just a little. "Nothing has to be decided tonight, does it?"

"No," she agreed. But she needed to make herself clear, she needed him to hear her. "But—"

"May I suggest to the committee chairwoman that we table this discussion until our next meeting?" His gentle look warmed her from within, even as he teased her. "That will give all parties time to reevaluate their positions."

"What if I can't change my position, Gabe?" She asked the question straight out. "What if I can't take the risk?"

He smiled right at her, the kind of endearing smile that had drawn her in from the beginning. "That just means I need to try harder, doesn't it?"

Oh, those words.

That look.

That smile.

She couldn't help but smile back. It felt wonderful to be wooed by a strong man who thought she was special. Who thought her children were special. She slid out of the booth and stood. Gabe followed. "Sure you don't want supper, Corinne? You've got to be hungry, and a few pieces of strudel aren't considered a meal. Plus I've got a built-in babysitter for the night. Wow, those are words I never thought I'd hear coming out of my mouth again."

She smiled and shook her head. "I've got to stop by Mom and Dad's and see the kids. But if you offer me supper tomorrow night..." She let the words float back to him as she walked to the door. "I will forgo my urge for strudel and enjoy a good meal. Pete and Kate are taking the kids into the city to see a holiday musical, so I'm on my own."

"I'd like that." He opened her car door for her once they were outside, then leaned down to hold her gaze. "See you in the morning."

She would see him then. And all day. And then for supper.

Suddenly the risk of the attraction seemed outweighed by the strength of the attraction, but was that the smart thing to do?

She didn't know. And until she did know, she should raise her guard, but when she was around Gabe Cutler, keeping her walls up was proving to be more than difficult.

It was next to impossible.

Chapter Eleven

"I can't believe we've lived on the lake all spring, summer and fall and we've only been on the water a few times." Tee flopped onto Kate and Pete's couch, thirty minutes later, grumbling. "That can't be right. Why do we live on the water if there's never time to take the boat out? And now it's supposed to get crazy cold and we'll pack it away until next spring."

"So much for having quality time with the kids," Kate whispered to Corinne. Louder she added, "I hear you, Tee. It can be tough in a big family like ours, especially with weddings and babies and new businesses opening up like we had this past year. It was a little crazy, wasn't it?"

Corinne's sister-in-law Rory and her new husband had adopted his late cousin's two small children when his mother passed away, Emily had purchased a bridal store and had a baby, and the oldest sister, Kimberly, was expecting her second child. For a family where not much had changed in a decade, so much had changed in the last eighteen months. "Next year won't be so wild. I don't think," Kate added. "Although I hadn't predicted this past year's increase in activity, so don't quote me on any of this."

"I'll have more free time next summer," Pete added from his recliner near the cozy fireplace.

"So will I," Corinne told them. "I'm going to step down as festival chairperson, to give me more time, Tee. I realized when we talked about this that I need to pay more attention to my current priorities. It's a good time for others to take over the civic stuff."

"You're sure about this, Corinne?" Kate slid a tray of very unhealthy cake squares her way, and Corinne took one.

"Yes. I want to do more things with Tee, and between Callan's baseball schedule and the festival meetings and follow-ups, Tee's getting left out." She met Tee's frown and blew her a kiss. "I will make this up to you, honey. I promise. I'm just sorry I was shortsighted this year."

"So we really have to put the boat away?"

"We should have taken care of it already.

Thanksgiving is coming up, which means another busy week."

"I can do it," Pete offered. "I'm happy to help."

"That would be great," Corinne told him before she waded in with a question she almost hated to ask. "About Thanksgiving..."

Kate looked up with interest.

Pete barely heard her—total male.

"We've got Gabe and the baby next door, and his family is almost four hours away. I don't think he should be alone for Thanksgiving."

Kate did exactly what Corinne was hoping she'd do. "Invite him here. There's plenty of space once we open the enclosed porch and plug in the heater. I expect he'd like that baby to be around other little ones, don't you?"

She did, but she had a more selfish reason for wanting Gabe to be comfortable around Dave's family. She wanted them to like him because she was sliding well past "like" when it came to her neighbor, and the Gallaghers had been her staunch support for years. Their acceptance of him meant a great deal to her. "That's fine with you?"

Kate held her gaze long enough to send a silent message of approval. "It's not only fine, honey. It's wonderful."

Heat stained her cheeks. She'd considered this attraction impossible for a long time, and the thought of new possibilities seemed wrong and right. The fact that she still hesitated added to her confusion.

"I'm going to bed." Tee didn't pause to kiss anyone good-night. She didn't look left or right. Corinne's funny, vibrant daughter trudged up the stairs looking tired and unhappy.

"Romance problems," Kate whispered once Tee was gone.

"She's twelve," Corinne whispered back. "We're not allowing her to think about boys for another four years. Do you think she missed the memo?"

Kate sent a rueful look toward the stairs. "Callan's friend Brandon was here today."

"She's crushing on him." Corinne scrunched her brow, because how did one handle this? She was out of her element, which meant she needed to figure this out. Quickly.

"He's nice as can be and paid her absolutely no attention while he and Callan arranged to go to the batting cages and the opening basketball game at the high school. Without her. We offered to take her, but her feelings were hurt at being left out. She and Callan used to do everything together, so his quest for independence is a touchy subject right now."

"I'll go talk to her." Corinne climbed the stairs. She found Tee in Kimberly's old room, a longtime favorite place to be at Grandma's house. "Hey. I didn't want to leave before saying good night to my best girl."

"G'night." Tee muttered the word, eyes pinched closed, much like she'd done as a baby. Only she wasn't a baby anymore.

"Tee." Corinne eased down on the side of the bed. "I really am sorry about the boat and the water and the stupid boys."

Tee's eyes flashed open. "I don't care about any of it. Not one speck. At all."

Corinne weighed Tee's declaration with a slight frown. "Even if you don't care, I'm still sorry. I won't let time get away from me again. I promise."

"Why are boys so dumb?"

"Are they all dumb?"

Tee sat up partway, eyes flashing. "I believe so."

Corinne had to laugh. "Oh, darling, they can be a frustrating lot, can't they? Why didn't you just go to the basketball game with your friends?"

Tee blew out a breath. "I was too mad. I had it all planned out."

Corinne waited for her to go on.

"Brandon was coming over, I knew they'd

want to go to the game, and I kept waiting and waiting for them to invite me. And they didn't."

"You could have invited yourself," Corinne reminded her. "Or just gone along and then you could have gone off with your friends from school."

"It wouldn't have been the same."

"The same as what you dreamed of?"

Tee flushed.

"If I say that Brandon's a clueless lout, that might make you feel better. But sometimes the person we're interested in just doesn't see us the same way, at the same time."

"The whole stupid 'He's So Not Into You' stuff," Tee declared. "So we wait?" Tee's brows shot up at the futility of that. "I hate waiting."

A trait from her father, absolutely. "Then don't wait. Shrug it off until the timing is better, honey. Give yourself some space. I'd hate to see you waste junior high on crushes when there's so much out there beyond boys. The romance thing will come, but I'd be okay if you gave it a little time. I think that would be the best thing to do, but not because I want to keep you a little kid. You only get one chance to be this age at this time. I'd like to see you enjoy it."

"And when Brandon does notice me, I'll ignore him completely and he'll regret his inattention the rest of his days."

"You've been reading *Anne of Green Gables*."

Tee nodded. "Anne and I have a lot in common, it seems."

"Oh, you do, darling." Corinne leaned down and hugged her too-eager-to-grow-up daughter. "And Anne turned out just fine, didn't she?" When Tee said yes, Corinne kissed her cheek. "And so will you. I'll see you Sunday, okay?"

"Yes. And Mom?"

Corinne stood. "Mmm-hmm?"

"Will I always be nervous and weird around boys? Because I hate that."

"No." Corinne shoved her personal reaction to Gabe aside. "No, you will be confident and self-assured. Eventually. I promise."

"Okay." Her beautiful, spunky daughter sank back down into the pillow. "G'night."

"Good night, darling."

Corinne closed the door softly. Regret pinged from within. She'd been foolish to let the nice weather get away from her, and more so to not take time with Tee. She'd do better next year, mostly because she really couldn't do worse.

Corinne.

Gabe shaved quickly the next morning, then

called next door. "Hey." He tried to sound casual when Corinne answered her phone, even though he felt anything but casual when thinking about her. "If we're having supper together tonight, it's silly to take two cars to the festival. How about we ride together?"

"What an absolutely sensible idea!"

Her teasing tone made him grin. "Can you be ready to leave in fifteen minutes?"

"I'm kidless so I'm ready now," she told him. "I'll walk over and see your mom and the baby for a few minutes."

"Perfect." He hadn't thought anything would seem perfect again, but opening up to Corinne had dulled his shadowed thoughts. She believed in him. Now if he could just learn to believe in himself. "See you shortly."

"I'm on my way."

He finished getting ready, rued another weekend gone without putting his boat up for the winter and hurried downstairs.

He paused, midstep.

Corinne was holding Jessie. Her soft blond hair shone beneath the overhead kitchen light, and the baby's pale skin made a contrast against Corinne's forest green turtleneck. The snug sweater and the infant's curve created a living portrait of motherhood.

She'd said she hated for this time in her life

to be over. She'd rued that plans had changed without her consent, years before.

The image of mother and child ramped up his heart. Maybe it didn't have to be over, for either of them.

She turned just then, spotted him and smiled. "This baby is intoxicating. I could snuggle her all day."

"She gets under your skin, that's for sure." He finished coming down the stairs and kissed the baby. "I'm pretty sure she flirts with me."

At that very moment, Jess peeked up at him and flashed a coy smile.

Corinne laughed. "She does! Oh, you sweet thing!" She nuzzled the baby's neck, making her laugh out loud, then handed her over to Gabe's mother. "Take her, Linda. Otherwise I'll stay right here where it's warm and cozy, just to get some baby time."

"I've got her." Linda shooed them toward the door. "Go make money for a good cause, and I'll see you after your date tonight."

"It's not a date," Corinne assured her.

Gabe grabbed his leather bomber jacket and gloves. "Thanks, Mom. Call me if you need me. And now that I've heard from the family court lawyer, I'll call Adrianna's parents. Might as well get things out in the open."

"Then I'm staying on hand," Linda declared,

"just in case they make the drive over here. When they get their minds set on the right or wrong of anything, they dig their heels in. My sister has never seen a shade of gray she liked," she added to Corinne. "She lives in a world of absolutes, and that can make a hard climate for raising children."

"See you tonight." Gabe kissed his mother, then the baby as Corinne went out the door. He shut the door firmly, made sure it was locked and climbed into the warming SUV.

"You heard back from the lawyer?"

He answered as he backed the car out onto the quiet road. "He sent me an email after examining the paperwork. He says Adrianna did all the right things. There is no father of record, and she acted responsibly in the best interests of her child. The fact that she revoked her parents' rights to custody in writing weighs against them, but I'm hoping they don't have to know she did that. There's been enough damage done already, from both sides. They kicked her out, knowing she was giving the baby up for adoption. I don't want to add more emotional injury to anyone's plate."

"Then why the concern that they might react badly to this? If they turned their backs on her, why would they do a quick turnaround?" Corinne wondered.

"Because it's me," he admitted. "My aunt has always been competitive. If my mother does something well, Aunt Maureen has to do it better. My mother raised me on her own, under a cloud of family backlash. In their minds, I turned out okay while both of Maureen's daughters have had successive problems. She's not going to like that Adrianna picked me because that means my mother did the better job of parenting. Stupid, right?"

"That's a competition with no winners, and too many losers," Corinne answered softly. "My mom was like that. I think that's why I bonded so well with Pete and Kate. They're so normal. They're strong but simple. And they're never in your face about things. I love them, and when I'm faced with a dilemma, I never think, 'What would my mother do?' I think, 'What would Kate do?' So I understand perfectly."

"Is your mother living?" He'd never heard her talk about family except the Gallaghers. There was so much he didn't know about her, but not nearly as much as he longed to know.

"No." She lifted her travel mug to sip her coffee, then didn't. "She died eight years ago. My grandparents raised me off and on. When she was sober, she'd take custody back. When she fell off the wagon, she'd let me live with them. I like that Adrianna has made a very tough decision by making this a clean break. She's put this baby first. My mother could never bring herself to do that, and it made for a wild ride when I was with her."

"I'm sorry, Corinne." He was, too. He'd gone into parenthood thinking it was a breeze when Grace was born. Life and experience had schooled him into a different reality. "But I'm glad you took the negatives and turned them into positives. It takes a lot of strength to do that, and you're amazing with those kids."

"Faith," she said softly. "My faith in God has been my solid ground. I'd have crashed and burned without that, Gabe."

He understood that, too. "It's my rock and my fortress. I hear you. Although sometimes I wonder what God thinks when my name crosses his desk? Does he see the darkness? Or does he focus on the light?"

"Oh, Gabe." She reached over and touched his cheek as he made the turn into a parking spot in the festival vendors area. "All he sees is the light of a good man who strives to be a better person, every day. He sees the pure light inside you, and I bet he wishes you could see it, too."

And just for a moment, he could. Turning,

looking into her eyes, seeing her pretty countenance, the look of trust…

In that instant he saw himself like she did, and it felt wonderful.

Chapter Twelve

She could do this, Corinne realized as they finished a quiet—and yes, *romantic*—dinner that night. With Gabe, she felt able to let her guard down. Maybe even to let go and let God rule the day, and cast her safety-first pledge aside.

The festival was over. The vendors had done well even with the shuttle buses running folks into the village. When she and Gabe had left to go to dinner, most of the vendors were loading excess goods into vans and trucks while wearing smiles of success.

That was good, but sitting here, having dinner with Gabe, laughing about funny incidents through the day...

This was wonderful and normal and she was pretty sure she'd be downright foolish not to grab hold of this man and then keep him, like say…forever?

The waiter brought their desserts in a to-go bag. Corinne shrugged into her coat as Gabe held it out. Then he tugged the sides together for her.

Her heart opened more, and she hadn't thought that possible. She held his gaze and covered one of his hands with her free one. "This was marvelous, Gabe."

He smiled down at her, his hands clutching the twin lapels of her coat. "Yeah?" His gaze dropped to her lips, and his smile grew. "I'm in total agreement." He moved closer.

Then he paused, winked and handed her the take-out bag of tiramisu. "Let's go check out that baby. I must be going soft on her because when I'm not there, I can't get her out of my mind. Even with my mother there."

"You're not going crazy overprotective, are you?"

He began to shake his head, then frowned slightly. "Possibly. But I'm working on it. I promise."

"Good." He reached around her to open the car door for her, then didn't. He paused instead.

Chill air surrounded them. The leaves had long since drifted from the trees, but twinkle lights took their place, marking the change of seasons and a month of holiday festivities.

He lowered his gaze again, and this time he didn't wait. Didn't hesitate. Didn't tease.

This time he gathered her in and took his own sweet time kissing her. A kiss that offered love and support with no words needed. A kiss that spoke to promises and pledges and so much more. And when he drew back, he laid his forehead against hers and whispered, "My lips like getting to know yours. They're so happy right now. Thank you for making them happy, Corinne."

She laughed and ducked her head against the smooth leather of his rugged jacket. It felt good to laugh in this man's arms, to be sheltered in his strong embrace, and when he kissed her again, Corinne was sure of one thing. She'd fallen head over heels for Gabe Cutler, and she wanted nothing more than to spend the rest of her life showing him that. And she was pretty sure he felt exactly the same way. She let herself get lost in the moment, because in Gabe's arms, she knew anything was possible, and Corinne hadn't felt that way in a long time.

A wonderful evening, full of possibilities of a new today and a better tomorrow.

He'd kissed his beautiful neighbor. He'd

taken his own sweet time kissing Corinne, and she'd kissed him back. He felt wonderful. Marvelous. Delightfully invigorated with new possibilities opening before him.

Corinne hit a Christmas music station on the radio as he pulled out onto the road. When she began to change it, he reached out a hand to stop her. "It's okay. I don't mind so much."

She slanted a smile his way, and the rusty hinges on his heart crept open wider. Her expression held hope and promise and affection. His courting skills were as rusty as his heart, but Gabe wasn't afraid to brush up on his skills with Corinne for however long it might take.

He'd been in love once, a long time ago.

Now he was falling in love again. He wanted everything right for her, and he was willing to do whatever it took to make that happen.

His tires hit a patch of black ice.

The car skidded sideways, then recovered. He gripped the wheel tightly, watching ahead for more rogue patches. Damp days and quick-chilling nights left drivers susceptible to ice slicks on country roads. Just as he thought that, the car ahead of them spun out of control.

The lights careened in a full circle, slid left, then right, then shot off the road, into a copse of tall, broad evergreens.

"Gabe!" Corinne's hand went to her mouth.

She grabbed for her phone instantly and hit 9-1-1. She was offering direction and location before he'd come to a full stop on the icy shoulder of the four-lane road.

"Don't stay in the car," he warned as he jumped out. "Just in case someone else spins out. And have Grant call out salt trucks ASAP."

Emily's husband Grant was the highway superintendent for Grace Haven. "I will." She climbed out of her side of the car as she made the call to her brother-in-law's cell phone.

Gabe rushed to the most accessible door of the damaged car, but the sedan was wedged between the trunks of two trees. Branches blocked his way and his vision. He'd grabbed his flashlight from the backseat, and wished it was the high-intensity model tacked to his service weapon. Still, it was better than nothing. He pulled branches back, but couldn't make progress on the door and hold the wide, draping spruce boughs at bay.

"I've got these." Corinne pulled the branches back, leaving him a clearer view. "I'll hold, you figure out how we can help them."

His light noted two passengers and a car seat.

His heart shoved up, into his throat. He pounded on the glass of the front door.

The air bags had deployed.

He detected movement on the far side. The driver was slumped, and the angle of the door's damage didn't allow Gabe access. He moved to the other side of the car.

Cars streamed by. A couple of them stopped. And in the distance, he heard the welcome sound of sirens. Backup was approaching.

The woman in the passenger's seat reached over and unlocked the door.

He pulled her door open. She struggled toward him, crying and gesturing. "My husband. He's not talking. He's not talking to me. Help him!"

"We will." Gabe guided her out. A man from a stopped car took Corinne's place at the branches, tugging them away from the vehicle.

Corinne circled the car and took the woman's arm. "Let's have a look, okay?"

The woman pushed away. "We have to get my husband out. I smell gas!"

Gabe smelled it, too. He reached in the passenger side, shut the engine down and hoped it was enough to prevent a fiery explosion.

"Can you get him out? Please, you have to help him!" Her tone begged and her face pleaded, and Gabe knew exactly how she felt. He knew it too well.

"Is the baby with you?" Gabe asked.

The woman squinted hard. "I don't think

so." She gripped her head. "My head hurts. It hurts so much." Pain contorted her features as she tried to answer his question. "No, she's with my mother. We were having a date night. Oh, no…" she wailed, as if re-realizing her husband's state while Gabe searched the man's neck for a pulse. When he felt the soft beat beneath the pads of two fingers, he sighed in relief.

"He's got a pulse. And help's coming." He called the words across the small grassy incline. Corinne had moved the woman into the clearing and was using the flashlight on her phone to check her over.

Sirens came closer. Flashing lights approached from both directions.

And then a car approaching from the north tried to brake quickly. It spun hard, just like the previous car had done.

The sleek coupe hit Gabe's SUV, did a three-sixty, bounced off Gabe's car again, then hurtled through the air, straight at the original vehicle. And Gabe.

Gabe took the ditch, headfirst.

The car sailed over him and into the stand of trees just in front of the first car.

He held his breath, certain that gravity was going to drop the car back into the ditch and take him out. When it sailed over his head, he made a leap for the embankment behind him and scrambled up the slick hill as if his life depended on it because it did.

The thick branches slowed the car enough to avoid hitting the tree trunks or the initial automobile, but then the car crashed down, into the ditch, onto the same hollow Gabe had sought as refuge.

He couldn't think about what might have been. There was no time for that.

He directed the EMTs and the firefighters with the Jaws of Life to the first car while he helped the driver and a little boy out of the second car.

He ran on adrenaline for nearly an hour.

At some point he noticed that Corinne was guiding the woman into an ambulance.

When the husband was finally extracted, a second ambulance took him to Rochester, where more serious injuries could be effectively treated.

Salt trucks peppered both sides of the road.

On-duty officers took statements.

Tow trucks arrived to clean up the extensive aftermath. The damage from the second accident left Gabe's SUV undrivable. Drew Slade and Grant McCarthy both showed up during the melee. "Gabe, you're not dressed for this. Go home," Drew told him. He motioned to Grant's SUV parked just up the road. "Corinne's in Grant's car. He'll drive you guys. Do you need to see a doctor? Did you get injured at all when that car went airborne?"

"Nothing," Gabe assured him. "I got out of the way in time."

"Then head home, I'll let you know how it all comes out. Corinne looks shaken up. I think she could use some warmth, peace and quiet right about now."

Of course she could, and he was so busy playing the hero that he'd lost track of her. What kind of man did that?

He strode to Grant's SUV and climbed into the backseat next to Corinne. "Hey. Are you okay? Are you warming up?"

She stayed on her side of the car and nodded. "Yes, Grant left the heater running and I'm thawing out. Any word on the injured?"

He shook his head as Grant swung the driver's door wide. "Drew said he'd let us know."

Grant settled into the driver's seat and eased the SUV onto the road. "Let's get you two home so you can relax. This was a crummy way to end a great festival weekend." He frowned at them through the rearview mirror. "But witnesses are calling both of you heroes. I'm glad you happened along when you did. And Corinne, thanks for the quick call.

That might have prevented a lot more problems tonight."

"It was Gabe's idea." Her voice was soft. She looked tired and worn. "Grant, can you drop me at Mom and Dad's place? I know they're at the musical, but I'd like to spend the night there. Be near the kids. And I texted them to watch out for black ice."

"Sure." He nodded and when they got into the town, he pulled into Kate and Pete's driveway.

Gabe got out to walk her to the door.

She waved him off. "It's fine, Gabe. You've had a rougher night than I did. I can let myself in."

Nerves tightened her tone. Her hands gripped her keys as if frozen to them.

"I'll just see you to the door, then."

"Okay." She walked forward, used the key and pushed the door open. "Good night."

She shut the door.

He stared at it, wishing they could decompress the evening together. As a cop, he understood the need to dissect a trauma, to talk about the good, the bad, the ugly…and then to put it behind you. He'd been able to do that in his professional life, if not his personal one.

He contemplated his options, then realized

it might be best to wait until tomorrow. She deserved a good night's sleep.

He didn't like the idea of walking away, but the closed door left few choices. He got back into Grant's vehicle, and when Grant dropped him off at the door, his mother was anxiously waiting for an update.

Jessie lay sound asleep in the crib. The lights were turned low, and the house next door sat black in the darkness. A night that began with such promise and light had turned dark in an instant.

He hugged his mother. "Let's talk in the morning, okay? I'm beat."

"Okay. I'll sleep by Jessie tonight. I don't mind a bit," she insisted, "and you've got a lot on your plate for tomorrow with Maureen and Blake."

He didn't refuse her kind offer. "I appreciate it, Mom. All of it."

She hugged him again, then reached up to kiss his cold, weathered cheek. "I know."

Chapter Thirteen

I can't do this. Not now. Not later. Not ever.

Corinne curled up in the corner of Rory's old bed, trying to get warm, trying to calm the gut-clenching fear that grabbed hold nearly three hours before and hadn't let go. No matter what she tried, she couldn't get the images out of her mind.

The coupe spinning out, ricocheting off Gabe's SUV, then sailing off the road, right at him.

Her heart had stopped while her pulse kicked into high. She'd run forward, wanting to save him, knowing she couldn't, and when the car settled and Gabe scrambled up the slope of the ditch, unharmed, she knew.

His death would paralyze her. His death would plunge her into depths of despair. Single mothers couldn't afford despair. They could barely afford to get sentimental over greeting card commercials because being a mom meant being on the job 24/7.

She clenched her hands, wanting to pray, but far too angry to find words.

She'd been so close to a new adventure, a new normal. So very close.

Was this God's way of showing her the dangers involved with loving a lawman? Or was it a test to see if she had what it took to be a trooper's wife?

She didn't.

She recognized that tonight.

Her heart ached. Her hands trembled, more with anger than fear, and her feet refused to warm up.

She'd nearly watched Gabe die, and it about did her in.

She'd overseen life-and-death situations in the crisis pregnancy unit often. She'd laughed and cried, prayed and comforted and was glad to do it.

But this…

She shuddered, replaying the scene in her head as the car sailed off the road. The look on Gabe's face, caught in the glow of airborne headlights. She saw him try to jump out of the way as the car blocked her view, then the long seconds of thinking the worst…

She stood and paced the room.

Sleep wouldn't come.

Her head ached from the intensity of it all.
What if he'd died?

But he didn't, her conscience scolded softly.

Corinne shrugged that off. Gabe was hero-quality. He didn't hesitate to pull that SUV over, and do what needed to be done. A deed that could have spelled his death sentence.

Would you prefer he pass people by? Would you want a man who drives on through, coolly calling 9-1-1 instead of pausing to help? And since when did life come with guarantees? Are we numbered by our timelines or God's?

She scowled.

God's, of course, but there was little use in tempting fate. And yet…

She loved that he waded into the fray instantly, that he took charge in order to save lives. Wasn't that what being a lawman was all about?

Yes.

But that didn't mean she could mentally and emotionally handle the possible outcomes, because tonight's emergency played in her mind like a broken record, spinning out of control. She'd pledged that she'd never live like that again.

Tonight's accident proved her right.

* * *

Aunt Maureen and Uncle Blake were on their way to Grace Haven, and they weren't happy. Were they coming to demand their granddaughter, or just complain that Gabe had her? He wasn't sure, but in either case, he wasn't about to subject the baby to a shouting match.

He tucked Jessie's car seat into the SUV and drove to the Gallaghers' house midday Sunday. Kate answered the door. "Gabe! Oh my gosh, come in and bring that little one with you. I think she's grown, Gabe!" She cooed to the baby as Gabe set the seat on the broad kitchen table. "What's up?"

"Is Corinne here?"

"She's not," Kate told him. She looked apologetic and worried all at once. "She took the kids shopping after church for some things they've been needing."

"Oh." Why did that seem odd to him? That she hadn't called or checked in or let him know? Mothers taking kids shopping was absolutely normal, especially on weekends. And yet… Something seemed amiss. "Kate, I know you're going to start watching Jessie tomorrow, but her grandparents are on their way from Saratoga and they're angry that I've got custody. I'm concerned that there might be a scene. Can you look after her this afternoon until the coast is clear?"

Pete came through the doorway leading to the front living room. "Are you expecting trouble?"

Gabe wasn't sure. "I'm preparing for the worst and hoping for the best. I've got Adrianna's paperwork, and the advice of an attorney, but I don't want Jess in the house when they arrive. They're angry and insulted, and my aunt tends to be melodramatic on a regular basis."

"No place for a baby, then." Kate released the seat belt clasps and lifted Jessie up. "Come here, sweetness." She nuzzled the baby's cheek, making her smile. "You go do what you have to do, Gabe. And if there's anything you need, just let us know."

"Do you want police backup?" As the former chief of police, Pete Gallagher never minced words.

Gabe shook his head. "My mother's there and I'm hoping we can sit down and talk things through. But in case it doesn't go like that, I want Jessie in a safe place."

"Sensible," Kate said. "We've got everything we need for a happy baby, and Sunday afternoon football, Gabe."

"Thank you. And can you have Corinne call me when she gets back?"

Kate's expression didn't quite match the cordial tone of her words. "Or you can pop next door later. I'm not sure if she's coming back here or heading straight home."

The feeling of unease crept farther up his back, but that could be anticipation of the upcoming standoff, too. Either way, he needed to get back to his place. "Right." He kissed Jessie goodbye and headed home, determined to make some kind of right out of too many wrongs.

A text from Mack came through as he pulled into his driveway. Taking Susie to ER. Something's wrong. Pray for us.

Grief flooded Gabe.

He sat in the car, head bowed, praying.

Mack and Susie had been his best friends since high school. They'd loved him throughout his losses, and as they'd tried to start a family of their own, he'd watched helplessly as their attempts came to nothing time and time again.

It made no sense. Why could his cousin conceive and deliver a healthy child while Mack and Susie met chronic failure? He texted back Praying! and he was, but the unfairness of it all angered him.

* * *

Don't look at Gabe's house.

Grab your bags and go straight in, eyes front.

Corinne followed her own directive, but when a text came through from Kate, it held a picture of a smiling baby curled up on Pete Gallagher's lap. Someone likes football! tagged the photo, and now Corinne looked toward Gabe's house.

A strange car sat in the driveway, parked crookedly across the asphalt.

Jessie's grandparents?

He'd said he was going to call them, and the baby had been removed from the house. Corinne had watched enough family dramas play out in the hospital to recognize the foresight in Gabe's preemptive strike. As she watched, his front door flew open.

A couple stormed out. The man banged a fist against a porch pillar, yelled, then strode to the car and slammed the door shut once he climbed in.

The woman stood, facing the door.

Was Gabe in the doorway? Or his mom?

Corinne couldn't see, but she read the anger and pain on the woman's face. Her mouth moved in quick fashion. Begging? Pleading? Yelling?

Corinne moved away from the window.

This wasn't her business. And after last night, she didn't dare make it her business. She'd been raised on family drama and hated it. She didn't want to face the angry woman, or the heroic man who'd narrowly escaped death the night before.

She wanted calm. She wanted structure and order, the peace and quiet she'd carefully orchestrated for years. How could she even consider risking that kind of loss for her kids?

"Mom! Can I run over to Coach's and ask him about the January schedule?" Callan half shouted the question as he loped toward the door. He spotted the woman on Gabe's porch and reconsidered his request. "On second thought, I'll wait. I can ask him on Thanksgiving."

Thanksgiving.

She'd invited Gabe to the Gallagher family meal and he'd accepted happily. Could she rescind the invitation?

Only a heartless creep would do that, but how could she spend a beautiful holiday with him under these circumstances? Especially a holiday based on faith and gratitude?

She couldn't. And yet, she had no choice. If she opted out of the family meal, her kids would think she'd gone crazy. Right about now, she wasn't sure she hadn't.

She put things away methodically, and when Gabe's footsteps sounded on the deck, her pulse sped up. She was scared to face him and afraid to lose him, two weak responses. How could she consider herself a strong woman if she allowed fear to guide her days? But was it fear? Or common sense because she'd lived through grievous loss once?

She sucked in a breath and crossed to swing open the door before he had a chance to knock. And the minute she saw his shell-shocked face, she grabbed hold of his big, strong hand and pulled him inside. "Come in, have some coffee and tell me what happened."

"I can't stay. I've got to get to Kate and Pete's and pick up Jessie." He frowned, facing her. "Corinne, about last night. We should talk about it. We shouldn't have left it like that and just gone our separate ways afterward. It was a stupid thing to do on my part, and I know better. I'm sorry."

Her heart shook harder than her hands, and both grew chill. "What was there to say, Gabe?"

He tipped his head in question.

"We were both there. We did what we could. And it looks like everyone is going to be okay, and I'm thrilled about that. You should be, too."

"I am." He spoke slowly, watching her make

busywork with her hands as she brewed his coffee. "What concerns me is your reaction, Corinne. You've barely looked at me since the accident. You haven't answered my texts—"

"Busy with the kids."

His frown lines deepened. "But I think the twelve-point-six seconds it takes to answer a text isn't the big deal you're making it out to be. Unless…" He took a step closer. "It is a big deal."

She couldn't do this.

She knew cops. She'd married one, her father-in-law had been one for decades and now her brother-in-law ran the police force. They were skilled in brushing off danger, shrugging off risk.

She possessed none of those skills, and she'd seen the risks Gabe was willing to take first-hand. She'd watched that car fly right over Gabe's beautiful, stubborn, thick head and felt the life drain right out of her until he scrambled up the opposite incline.

Her gut recoiled, remembering.

She forced her hands to stop shaking by clutching her mug. "Gabe, we've been friends for a long time. We've worked together on the baseball team and the festival. We like each other."

Her words disappointed him. She read it in his face, and in the set of his shoulders.

"But I have to keep my focus on raising my two kids for the next five years. They have to be my first priority. I'm sure you can understand that better than most."

"You're tired."

She started to argue, but she couldn't. He was correct. She was tired of being alone, of running the show, of missing the sweet things that seemed so near last evening. What if they'd passed through that slicked-up area two minutes before? None of this would have happened, and she'd be in this man's arms right now.

But it *did* happen, and her reaction was an eye-opener and a deal breaker.

"You want to brush me off."

That sounded harsh. She winced.

"All right. I get it." He didn't reach for the coffee. "But what I don't get is why everything changed. What turned everything upside-down. And while I'd love to have time to get to the bottom of it, Jessie's grandparents have just reminded me that my carelessness took the life of one little girl…"

Could his aunt and uncle really have said such a thing? She reached out a hand to his arm. He moved back just enough to avoid the touch, and that tiny action pained her heart.

"They wanted to face me personally to let me know that they're disgusted by their daughter's choices yet again, but also that they have no interest in raising a child born of sin, and they'll make sure everyone in the family knows she's a tainted child. No big news there, right? On that note, I'm going to drive into town, pick up that precious baby and take care of her." He didn't wait for her to reply.

He strode to the door, head down.

She wanted him to hesitate. She longed for him to dissemble her fears, tease her out of her funk and move on through life together.

He did none of those things.

He stepped through the door, pulled it gently shut behind him and crossed the deck.

He didn't look back. Not once.

Her chest ached.

Tears filled her eyes, then rolled down her cheeks.

Tee was studying.

Callan was watching football and pretending to do homework.

And here she was alone, again, by her own doing.

The rights and wrongs didn't matter at the moment. Not when the hollowness in her chest weighed her down.

She reached for her phone to call him, then stopped.

This was what she wanted, wasn't it? She'd

pulled back purposely with this result in mind, a measure of firm separation between her and the man she'd come to love so dearly.

She'd forgotten how real the pain of separation could be.

A car cruised by her front windows, driving slowly toward the town. Gabe, going to pick up the baby and bring her home.

"...my carelessness cost the life of one little girl..."

How could they have thrown that up to him?

And how could you not offer comfort and warmth upon hearing it? You stood here, knowing how that must have hurt, and did nothing to assuage his guilt.

She dumped her coffee into the sink.

Her laptop buzzed messages repeatedly, follow-ups to the well-orchestrated festival. She slipped to the floor, drew the computer into her lap and answered each one with false cheer.

Yes, the festival had been a great success. But what seemed important a few months ago dimmed in the glow of real-life issues.

For a little while she'd moved forward, thrilled with the idea of having it all. But now...

She swallowed a sigh, bit her lip and kept right on pretending everything was all right as she answered questions and posts about the Christkindl.

She'd get by, like she'd been doing for so long. Only now it seemed like a shallow shadow of how sweet life could be if only she was brave enough to live it. But in her heart and in her soul Corinne was pretty sure she lacked the courage Gabe needed in a woman. And that wasn't good for either of them.

Another miscarriage. Staying strong for Susie. Trying anyway. Heartbroken again.

Gabe wanted to throw the phone at the text from Mack.

He wanted to rail at God, at life, at fate, at whatever governed the stupidity of parenting and infertility. His friends had been so close to the dream they'd been chasing for years.

I'm so sorry. So dreadfully sorry. He texted the words back as Jessie slept in her little padded crib.

I know you are. That message came through. Several seconds later another one followed. Us, too.

Gabe's heart broke for them. He got things ready for the morning, and made sure everything was in order for an overnight bottle. Jessie was quite predictable that way. The thought of eight hours of sleep clearly meant nothing to her.

He didn't look out his window.

He tried not to think about Corinne next door, about Callan and Tee, so full of life. She'd shrugged him off, and the standoff with Maureen and Blake had left him unnerved.

How could people be that way? He didn't know, but there was only so much rejection he could handle in one day. He stretched out on the couch, and didn't turn on the late game. He needed sleep because tomorrow was a work-day. When he didn't doze off, he shut his eyes and pretended to rest. With his eyes closed, he had no reminders of the beautiful family next door, or those kisses the night before. But even with his eyes deliberately shut, he couldn't get Corinne out of his mind, and sleep was a long time coming.

Chapter Fourteen

Corinne spotted Susie's name on the patient roster the next morning.

No.

Susie was solidly into her second trimester, further than she'd ever gotten before. Two days ago she'd been wide-eyed with hope, and now she was tucked in the crisis pregnancy unit of the third floor.

Corinne set her purse and folders down and hurried to room 3102. She scanned the notes at the nurse's station, then approached the room, heart-heavy. "Hey."

"Corinne." Sorrow filled Susie's red-rimmed eyes. Mack's were no better. "I was so hopeful this time."

"I know." Corinne sank onto the small stool alongside the bed and took Susie's hand. She had no words of comfort for the heartbroken couple. In this line of work, you either won the race or you didn't. There was no second prize. "I'm so sorry."

Mack's chest heaved.

Susie gazed up at him with such a look of love and loss that Corinne's eyes filled, seeing it. "We've been here before, darling. And we've always gotten through. This time's no different."

He clutched her hand, and leaned down. "I am so mad at God right now. I can't even describe it, Susie." He clamped his lips tight, trying to hold back a torrent of emotion.

"God doesn't do this," Susie whispered, holding his gaze. She squeezed his hand lightly. "God wants us happy, Mack, but bodies are imperfect vessels. For some reason, mine doesn't work right when it comes to babies."

"Don't take this on yourself." Mack bent and pressed a kiss to Susie's flushed cheek.

"I'm not," she whispered. "I've done that in the past and it's gotten us nowhere. There's no time to sit around and cast blame, is there? Not when there's so much suffering in the world. We'll get through this, with God's help. And with each other."

He hugged her, swiped a big ol' trooper hand to his streaming eyes, and nodded. "We will, honey. We will."

"Mack, can you get me a cup of tea?" she asked. "That orange tea would be nice. The spiced one."

"Sure."

He left, almost glad for something helpful to do, and when he'd disappeared through the door, Susie broke down.

Corinne slipped onto the side of the bed and held her.

How hard her job was in moments like this.

She celebrated the triumphs of modern medicine and healthy babies under crushing circumstances, but this…the loss of a planned-for infant, the loss of a blessed child…

Oh, her heart ached for them right now.

Susie pulled back and grabbed a stash of tissues. "I don't want Mack to see me like this. We were so excited, Corinne." She smiled through red-rimmed eyes. "Halfway there, and then…"

"I know." Susie's report indicated no fetal heartbeat as of Sunday night. So now they waited for the inevitable.

"I wish this baby had a chance to know us."

Corinne's heart gripped tight. She'd felt the same way with Tee and Dave, two souls, passing in the night, with never a chance to speak.

"I'd have told him what a great dad he had. How amazing Mack is, how brave and strong and true. How I can count on him in every way. Oh, Corinne, I'd have given anything just to have a chance to tell my baby son what an amazing man his father is. Do you think he knew? Someway, somehow, in his little baby haven? Did he know how much we loved him?"

"I'm sure he did." She whispered the words of comfort and held Susie's hand. "I'm sure he knows it now, as well, tucked in the arms of our Savior. And I don't have any pretty words, Susie, and no way to make this better, but I truly believe that your son knows you and you'll know him one day. Pure and perfect, in God's kingdom. And he'll be yours forevermore."

Footsteps sounded in the hallway.

Mack came in, carrying Susie's tea. "One sugar and no lemon."

"Perfect, Mack. Thank you."

Corinne stood. "I've got a meeting coming up, but I'm available the rest of the day. Let me know if you need anything, okay? Anything at all."

They nodded, but Corinne understood the truth better than most. The one thing they needed was a successful pregnancy, and that had been denied again.

She waded through the day, and then the night, and then the day again.

She didn't want to celebrate Thanksgiving

this week. She didn't want to pretend she was grateful when she was mostly angry.

She felt like a fake, talking to Kate about pies and cranberry relish. She didn't care about it, about any of it. Not right now.

Susie was discharged late Tuesday, going home with empty arms and womb.

Gabe was doing a good job of avoiding his closest neighbor, and his absence only exacerbated the ache in her soul.

And Tee was trying to figure out what to do with the half day off before Thanksgiving. Callan was spending the afternoon at a friend's, and Tee grudgingly decided to work on her long-term history project while home alone. "Although I don't know why I can't do something fun," she grumbled Tuesday night. "Callan gets to do whatever he wants and I get to come home alone. Again."

"You don't have to come home and work on history," Corinne reminded her. "You could go to Grandma's house and help with the babies. She'll have Jessie there, and Aunt Kimberly is bringing Davy over so she can help Grandma with the squash and sweet potato casserole."

"I hate sweet potato casserole."

That wasn't the point, but Corinne let it slide. "But you love babies."

Tee stared out, into the night, then shrugged.

"I wanted to go to Melody's house, but they've got to drive to Cooperstown to be with family. And Gen's family is going to visit her grandpa in a nursing home for a holiday thing. And you said I couldn't go to Jason's house and hang out with them."

"I don't know Jason and I don't know his parents, Tee."

"I know him. That should be enough," Tee spouted. "If you trusted my judgment."

"It's not about trusting you, it's about being a responsible parent and keeping my daughter safe."

Tee sighed.

"Should we turn on the lights?" Switching on the monstrous array of outdoor Christmas lights wouldn't fix Tee's conundrum, but it might brighten the dark night stretching far beyond their windows. "I know we usually wait until Thanksgiving, but I think we're close enough. Don't you?" She went outside and plugged in the solar-activated displays.

The yard sprang to life around her. Merry lights chased along the dock, and twinkle lights gleamed from the roofline. Ground spotlights illuminated the glowing family of deer and the beautiful Nativity set while Snoopy and Woodstock inflated in the front yard.

When she went inside, Tee had disappeared

upstairs. Was she peeking out the window at the fun-filled yard? Or was she moping on her bed? At twelve years old, Tee needed to learn to deal with things a little better. Sure, life wasn't always the way you wanted it to be, but part of growing up was developing a thick skin and moving on. She'd have fun at Kate's house. They both knew that, but Tee was stubborn enough—and mad enough—to obstinately choose to come home on her own, and it wouldn't surprise Corinne if she did exactly that.

As she drove into work on Wednesday morning, it seemed like the simple joys of Thanksgiving had escaped her and she had no idea how to get them back.

Maybe it's time to ease up on the reins. To take a step back and let life unfurl as it should. You don't have to control everything. Do you?

She never used to, she realized as an unusually warm sun bathed her car. A weak jet stream had been pushed high by a strong warm front out of the Deep South, a front that would be pushed east quickly by an approaching Midwest winter storm system. But for now the day dawned warm and dry for late November, a true surprise. Who expected T-shirt weather in late November? No one in Central New York, and yet the reality surrounded her.

Things had changed on that fateful day that took her husband's life. She'd worked hard to raise normal, grounded children, rich in faith and hope, but she'd stood guard all the while.

Now they were chomping at the bit for more freedom, and that unnerved her a little. Some days, more than a little.

Dear God...

She started the prayer and didn't finish it.

Her faith had been her stronghold through so much, but even that felt threatened recently. Was that her fault?

She pulled into the staff parking area, flashed her badge to security and took the elevator upstairs. Tonight she'd bake a pie and make cranberry relish and pretend everything was all right. It wasn't, but she had years of pretending under her belt. She'd gotten quite good at it, thank you very much.

"Where are you spending Thanksgiving?" Gabe's mother had called first thing Wednesday morning to see how everything was going. She'd called every day, just to touch base, the kind of thing that mothers do when distance creates concern. "That nice family next door? Or should I come up there and spend Thanksgiving with you? I can cook turkey there as easily as I can cook it here, Gabe."

Gabe sidestepped her hints with an agility refined by years of his mother's matchmaking. "We're having dinner at the Gallaghers' house. The folks who've been watching Jessie for me."

"Good," she said. She knew they were Corinne's family, and that seemed to please her. There was no way in the world he could tell her that Corinne had moved herself out of the picture completely, mostly because he didn't want to believe it himself. "And how are Mack and Susie doing? Are they all right?"

His lungs went tight. He had to pause before answering, long enough to gather his wits and his breath. "Like you'd expect. Heartbroken and disappointed that they got so close to their dream and had it snatched away again."

"Miscarriages are like that," she answered softly. "There's so much silent loss and guilt involved. I'm heartbroken that this happened again, Gabe. It's an awful wound for them."

It was.

He'd visited Susie and Mack in the hospital. He'd watched his best friend cry when they pretended to go for a walk to let Susie rest. And he'd gotten teary-eyed right along with Mack.

They didn't deserve these constant failures, and yet Susie refused to blame God or take out her anger on others.

Kate's phone buzzed into his Bluetooth. "Gabe, I know you were going to pick Jess up early, but she just fell asleep. Why don't you leave her here for a couple of hours and let her get a good nap in?"

"You don't mind?" he asked, but he already knew the answer.

"Not at all! Waking a sleeping baby goes against everything I believe in. I'll call you when she wakes up, and that'll give me time to feed her before you get here."

"Perfect. I'll take this couple of hours to drain the boat's oil and get it put up for the winter."

"Pete was going to do Corinne's, but hasn't gotten over there yet. Maybe I'll send him along to join you," she suggested. "We'll get them both done and he won't be underfoot while we get the squash baked for tomorrow."

He heard Pete's laugh in the background, followed by his voice. "I can take a hint, and you couldn't ask for a nicer day to get this done. Tell Gabe I'll be at the lake in about fifteen minutes."

"I heard him," Gabe told her. "Thanks, Kate."

"No problem."

He hung up the phone, pulled into his drive and changed into old clothes quickly. He had just enough time to grab coffee before Pete pulled in next door. "Hey, Pete. You want coffee before we get started?"

"Don't mind if I do." Pete moved his way and held out a travel mug. "We can make it right in here and I'll drink it while we take care of these boats. The weather's about to change on us, and I'll be mad at myself for not taking care of things I should have done weeks ago. With that storm approaching, we're on borrowed time as it is."

"Our sweet reprieve today is coming to an end," Gabe agreed. "The storm front is moving in fast, according to the radio." He filled Pete's travel mug. Thick gray clouds had started to approach from the west, and when the wind licked the curtains with a distinct chill, he closed the front window and headed toward the door. "Let's get this done."

Gabe stepped outside.

He stopped, stared, then pointed. "Did you move Corinne's boat?"

Pete came through behind him. His gaze followed the direction of Gabe's hand. "No, of course not. I just got here. Do you think someone stole it?"

A wave of wind came through again, a gust

that meant the early-day respite of warmth was drawing to a swift end. "Tee."

Pete went pale. "You think she took the boat out?"

"She had this afternoon off, right? And Callan texted me that he and Brandon and Tyler were going to the batting cages to stay in shape."

Pete raced for the shore, peering out across the blue-gray water. "I don't see her, and we've got choppy conditions already."

"Call Corinne. Make sure she didn't hide the boat someplace before we panic."

Pete hit Speed Dial on his cell phone, then scowled. "It's dead."

"I'll call." Gabe hit the number, praying she'd answer. She'd ignored his text messages, but he couldn't afford her fear to mess up this call. This one was too important.

No answer.

He flipped to text, hit her number and put in 9-1-1. Answer ASAP.

And then he called again.

"Gabe, what's wrong? What's happened? Is Jessie all right?"

Her voice was worried for him, worried for that beautiful baby when she should be concerned for her precocious, headstrong daughter. "Corinne, where's your boat?"

"In the yard where I left it." Her voice sounded pragmatic at first, but he could tell when she put one and one together. "Gabe. Tee's home for a half day, working on a project. Is she in the house?"

Her tone had changed completely, because she knew the answer before she asked the question. "Did she take that boat out alone, Gabe? With a storm coming?"

"Pete just checked the house. There are lights on, and her laptop is open on the table, but the boat key isn't on the rack. She's gone and the boat's gone."

"Aaarrrggghhh!" He heard a door close, then another. "I'm on my way, but Gabe, by the time I drive home, the weather will have changed. It's already snowing here, and I'm thirty minutes west of you guys." He heard her call out an emergency goodbye to the charge nurse at the desk. "I can't get there in time to make a difference."

"Pete's here, we'll go after her in my boat. Call it in so I don't wear my battery down or lose a signal. Give them the address, her favorite spots and the boat description. Tell them anything you can tell them to help locate her. She's a strong swimmer and she knows to wear a life vest. The sheriff's department will send their boat patrol. So will Grace Haven. But hurry, Corinne. Hurry."

She didn't have to be told twice.

She called in the emergency, then called Drew directly. Drew knew Tee. He'd be able to advise where the water rescue patrol should launch to minimize search time.

Tee...

She couldn't let herself cry.

She couldn't let herself come undone.

There would be plenty of time for that later, when Tee was safe and sound and grumbling about boys, school and anything else that messed up an adolescent girl's love of life.

She should have taken the kids out on the water more. She knew that, and the truth came roaring back now. She'd spent her time trying to be everything to everyone and forgot to prioritize her daughter's love of the water. Of boating and tubing and fishing. And how much she loved going out with her grandpa.

For years Tee had been dragged to game after game to support her big brother's love of baseball. How had she been so careless with Tee's hopes and desires? She ran to her car, headed for the interstate and got instantly bogged down in pre–Thanksgiving Day traffic, slowed by the thickening snow.

Kate called just as Corinne realized her predicament. "I'm talking you home so you don't lose it on the way," her mother-in-law announced when Corinne took the call on the car's hands-free phone system. "It's a terrible day to hurry anywhere, Corinne, especially with the weather and holiday traffic."

She'd found that out, and should have stayed off the interstate. Why hadn't she considered that before taking the entrance? Because she was scared. Scared for her daughter and scared for Tee's safety, and she was over twenty miles away, unable to do a thing about it. "I can't believe this, Mom. Tee taking the boat out alone. The traffic. The snow. Any of it."

"I love that Tee is so much like her father," Kate replied softly. "She's Dave, through and through. But in times like this I wish she had a little more of you in her. That hint of caution."

Corinne bit her lip because what used to be caution had become fear somewhere along the way. "Have you heard from them? Anything?"

"Nothing yet. Gabe took his boat out and Dad's at your place in case she makes it back there. They wanted someone to be at home base."

Oh, Tee...

Her heart ached. Her hands trembled. Why hadn't she paid more attention to her daughter?

She was so busy being cautious that she forgot to let Tee be Tee. "I can't stand the thought of something happening to her." She whispered the words around the hard swell of her throat. "I can't even imagine my life without her, Mom."

"Then, don't." Kate stayed strong and simple, qualities she exampled every day. "Imagine how we're going to celebrate Thanksgiving with her safe return, and all the stories we'll have to tell. If we don't kill her first once they get her back to shore."

"You think they will? Get to her in time? Get her back safely?" There. She said it.

She'd lived on the water for a lot of years. She understood how quickly a calm lake could become a dangerous thing, and the slanted snow and strong winds surrounding her meant visibility would diminish rapidly. Creeping along the short stretch of interstate, she could barely see two car lengths ahead. How could Gabe and the others possibly find Tee on the lake in these conditions?

"I think Jesus has calmed the waters before. He can do it now." Kate's voice was both firm and gentle. "I'm placing our girl and these rescuers in God's hands, Corinne. And the fact that Tee loves the water and has a knack for handling anything she tackles."

"Like her father."

"Yes."

Awareness broadsided her as she crept along in bumper-to-bumper traffic. "I tried to keep her safe by clipping her wings. Not letting her be herself, not letting her fly free. And I probably put her in more danger because of it."

Kate laughed lightly. "Oh, Corinne. Kids like Tee and her father will always find danger. It's their nature. But their fearlessness is also their strength. They're not timid, or intimidated by much of anything. Although I'm pretty sure that David inspired every gray hair I have. Well, Kimberly gave me her share, too. Rory and Emily were almost a relief by comparison."

Corinne understood completely. Kimberly and Dave were always ready to take the plunge into anything and everything. That aptly described her daughter, too. "Will you pray with me, Mom?"

Kate exhaled a soft breath into the phone, then said, "I'd be happy to."

Chapter Fifteen

Gabe scoured several eastern-shore coves at their end of the long, tapering lake, but didn't see Corinne's boat.

Would Tee have had sense enough to seek the far shore as the storm rolled in? Or would she try to make it back home?

She'd aim for home, he decided. Mostly because she'd get in huge trouble for taking the boat out on her own, but also because she was Tee. If it looked like a challenge, she was the first one on board.

He gunned the engine, heading south, binoculars raised. The wind sliced across the lake, bearing straight east. The drop in temperature was record-setting, even for Central New York. Pete would call him if Tee showed up back home, but as the first snowflakes began to fall, Gabe understood the seriousness of the worsening conditions. He needed to find her soon and get her home, warm, safe and dry.

He headed east, then slowed the engine.

Tee loved boating. More than that she loved fishing. She'd fished with Corinne's grandfather when he was alive, so maybe taking the boat out wasn't so much of a joy ride as it was a way to remember those special times with her great-grandpa.

He turned southwest, aiming for Caldecott Beach. Fish liked to hang out in the warmer, shallower waters a quarter mile out of the rocky cove marking the hotel's sandy beach. Buoys marked the dredged channel, allowing boats to tie up at the Caldecott Hotel docks, but with the rising chop and snow, the buoys wouldn't be visible. That meant Tee had nowhere to go but home, and that was a long ride north in these conditions.

He thought he'd see the rescue boats manning the waters from multiple directions.

He saw nothing as visibility and temperature dropped moment to moment.

He used his navigation system to guide him toward Caldecott. If he drifted too near the shore, he'd hit those rocks himself. If he stayed too far out, he might miss Tee altogether, if she was here. He could only pray that if she wasn't here, that one of the other boats would find her and haul her into safety.

He slowed the motor just enough to churn through the water and called Drew. "I'm at Caldecott. Where are you guys?"

"South of you, Meyering's Cove, heading east."

"Anything?"

"No. And with the decreasing visibility, we're flying blind."

"I'm moving slow. Chop's increasing."

"Watch those rocks."

"Roger." He hung up the phone, scanning as best he could.

He thought he'd hear her motor.

He heard nothing over the slap of waves and the increasing wind. Visibility had gone minimal, but his location system had him coasting into the fishing nook area. He dulled the engine and yelled, "Tee! Can you hear me?"

Nothing.

He crept forward, praying with every passing moment, then again yelled, "Tee! Tee, can you hear me?"

Still nothing.

He started to turn, then paused, feeling stupid.

The horn. He hit the horn three times, quickly. He paused, waiting. Just as he was about to turn outward, he heard something ahead and to the right. Near the rocky outcroppings. Three short beeps. Three long. Three short. They were faint, but they were audible.

S.O.S.

He answered with three short beeps again, and edged her way, praying she'd repeat the signal.

She did, and it was louder this time, which meant he was getting closer.

"Tee!" He yelled her name repeatedly, wanting to see her. To grab hold of her and take care of her and return her to her mother, safe and sound. He hit the horn again, and when she replied with the S.O.S. signal, Corinne's boat appeared before him almost instantly, off to his right. "I've got you, honey. Grab hold of this." He threw her a rope. "Tie it down so I can come alongside."

She was scared, soaked and cold. He watched her try to maneuver the rope to no avail. Time for plan B. "Are you anchored?" He raised his anchor to help her understand the question over the sound of the wind and water slapping waves against her boat.

She frowned, then nodded.

"Okay." He couldn't command two boats back to safety. He knew his vessel better, but he couldn't risk getting Tee on board, even with her life jacket on. If someone needed to switch up boats, it was him, and it was now. He stuffed his cell phone and his waterproof flashlight into the coat pocket of an old extra coat he kept stowed in the boat hatch. He threw the coat to her, then did the same with his jacket. He kicked off his shoes, anchored his boat and jumped into the water.

Weight pulled him down. The cold water made him suck a breath. He pushed back up, spitting and sputtering, spotted Tee's boat and swam her way. The wind and waves doubled his work.

He cut the angle, finally got alongside and reached up. Now he needed to board her boat without tipping them—and the boat—into the water.

She reached out a hand with such a look of determination, he grabbed hold, and with her balance and his effort, he heaved himself up and in.

He stared up at her for a few seconds, then flashed her a grin. "Catch any fish?"

"Oh, Coach." She threw herself at him as he scrambled up. "I'm so dumb! I just wanted to…" Uncontrolled shivering stole her words away, but he got the gist.

"Put that coat on and sit right there. We're going to get back to safety. Grab my torchlight and aim it toward the water in front of the boat, to the right side."

She tugged the coat on. He helped her zip it when her hands refused to work, and then she held the strong, waterproof flashlight as steady as she could with chilled hands while he pulled his jacket back on.

He aimed for the hotel.

He'd fished out here several times over the years, but not often enough to remember the channel buoys. He turned the boat into the snow but lost his bearings instantly and re-thought his choices.

He couldn't chance it. He was more familiar with the northern end. He'd have to make the wild ride back there and pray them to safety. He turned about, increased the motor and pointed north. "We're going home, kid."

She nodded, too cold to talk.

He headed north, praying silently, hoping for just enough of a break in the snow that he could spot houses, lights or a spot to pull up. He watched the speedometer and the gas gauge. It was tipping to the left, getting dangerously low. He tried to reach Drew.

Nothing.

He couldn't text and drive the boat at the same time.

He tried Corinne's number, and she answered immediately. "Gabe? Where are you?"

"I've got her." He had the phone tucked against his shoulder. "We're low on fuel, we're heading your way, alert Drew and all law enforcement, whoever you can contact. I'm snowblind, but I should be getting close. I think."

"We lit a fire."

"You what?" He couldn't have heard that right.

"On the shore. We lit a fire on the beach to help guide you in. Grandpa taught me that. Watch for it, Gabe. It's pretty big."

She'd no more than said the words when he spotted an orange haze behind them, to his left. He'd gone past their beach, and if his call hadn't gone through, he'd still be searching. "I've got it. Coming about. We're not going to try to dock. I'm running aground."

"I'm praying you in safely."

Those words. The gentleness in her tone.

He couldn't think about that, or let it mean too much. She'd made herself clear, and he had a lot of his own reckoning to manage. Nothing like a near-death experience to reevaluate just about everything there was in life that matters.

"Hunker down, Tee, just in case we bump hard." She followed his shouted direction, peering at the fire ahead.

The wind didn't allow the luxury of coasting in. He'd have to go aground swift and hard, then cut the engine, and that's exactly what he did.

He pitched forward. His head took a nasty shot from the windshield, but Tee stayed tucked between the seats without a scratch from their hard landing.

People streamed forth.

EMTs helped them from the boat. Tee's legs buckled the moment she tried to stand. They called for a stretcher, but she'd been cold too long already.

Gabe rounded the hull, lifted her up and carried her to the waiting ambulance. Corinne raced to them. She gripped Tee's hand. "Come on, sweetness, let's get you warmed up, okay?"

Tee blinked up at her mother. Her eyes mixed sorrow and joy. "I'm s-sorry, M-Mom." Shivers grabbed hold as she tried to speak again.

"We'll save the apologies for later, okay?" Corinne climbed into the ambulance as the medics took over. "Right now let's just get you warmed up."

He backed away, letting mother and daughter have their moment.

Corinne turned and put a hand out. "Gabe."

She wanted to thank him.

He saw it in her face, her gaze.

He didn't need thanks. He'd done exactly what he had to do, answering the pledge he'd made long years before.

He lifted his hand. "I'll see you later. I want to make sure everyone gets in all right. And you." He leaned in far enough so Tee could see him. "Drag me along on your next fishing trip, okay? I guarantee we'll have better luck together than you do on your own."

She tried to smile as silent tears rolled down her chilled white cheeks. "Okay."

He moved back and closed the rescue wagon doors.

Tee needed warmth and time with her mother. A trip to Grace Haven Memorial would give her both.

He scrubbed a hand to his face.

Pete called to him from inside, but he couldn't face questions right now. When Drew called in the "all clear" that all units had made it out of the water, Gabe trudged back to his house.

Pete and Callan had doused the fire with the garden hose and sand while reporters snapped pictures left and right.

Medics wanted to take Gabe in and check him out.

He refused.

He was fine, or would be once he got out of

the frigid wet clothes. His long, cold boat ride had given him time to assess a few things. Now he needed enough faith and courage to see those things through.

"Mom, I am so sorry." It was after ten when a very contrite Tee appeared on the stairs facing the kitchen on Thanksgiving morning.

Relief flooded Corinne the moment she spotted her beautiful girl. Tee looked so much better than she had fifteen hours before.

Fear had struck an arrow into Corinne's heart yesterday, a sharp piercing of how quickly life could change, a lesson she'd thought she'd learned a long time ago. But life hadn't changed because Gabe Cutler was brave enough to rush to a kid's rescue when needed.

She hated herself for thinking his raw courage could be a bad thing after the car accident.

If Gabe wasn't strong and brave and true, she might not have a daughter today. She owed Gabe an apology at the very least, and maybe...just maybe...he'd give her the second chance to be the brave woman she'd claimed to be long years ago.

"Is that apple pie I smell?"

"It is." Corinne pointed to the island behind her. "I made a little one, just for you, for breakfast."

"Pie for breakfast?" That thought relieved Tee's features quickly. "With ice cream?"

"If you'd like." She finished grinding the cranberries and nodded to the oranges. "I'm going to have you finish this up for me, okay? And then we'll talk about how I'm going to lock you in your room for four or five years until common sense prevails. But I'll save that lecture until after the cranberry-orange relish is ready."

Tee crossed the room and hugged her tight. "I will never do something that stupid again. I was so mad that we live on the water and almost never take the boat out. I felt like I never get to just sit and fish since Great-Grandpa died. And the weather was so beautiful." She sighed and laid her head against Corinne's shoulder. "I'm so sorry, Mom. You can lock me away. I deserve it."

"How come I get All-County in baseball and you get the newspaper headlines?" Callan pretended to be insulted as he came in with an armload of firewood and the daily paper. "You're all over the news, Tee. Well. You and Coach."

"We're in the paper?" She squealed softly, then shifted gears again, total Tee. "I have to thank Coach. He knew where to come because we talked about it before, and he sacrificed his boat. I've got to pay him back, somehow. I can't believe he did that for me, Mom." She raised her gaze to Corinne's. "He didn't even hesitate, he just jumped into the water, came aboard and brought me home."

"Well, that's how Coach is," Callan offered. He slung his arm around Tee and gave her a sideways hug. "He always puts the other guy first. That's where I learned it from." He shrugged. "Glad you're okay." He tipped his gaze down to Tee. "But try not to do anything stupid again. At least for a while. Okay?"

"Deal. And I'll figure things out with Coach at Grandma's today. Should I save him some of my pie?" She looked back at Corinne, and Corinne shook her head.

"I made another one for dessert. I'll make sure he gets some."

"Okay." She took the pie into the living room and turned on the Thanksgiving Day Parade, and for a few minutes she was the little girl Corinne had worked so hard to raise alone.

But she wasn't that little girl anymore. She was almost a teenager, and Corinne had been so busy trying to be perfect, she'd forgotten how important it was to just "be."

God and Gabe had given her a second

chance yesterday evening. One way or another she wanted to make the very best of this new opportunity.

Chapter Sixteen

Gabe knocked at Susie and Mack's door shortly before eleven on Thanksgiving morning. He had a diaper bag slung over one shoulder as Jessie gurgled and batted her hands in the car carrier he clutched in the opposite hand.

Mack opened the door. He looked tired at first glance, but when he saw it was Gabe, he threw the door wide. "Come on in, we'll give you a hero's welcome! I'm so glad you're all right, man!" Mack clapped him on the back as Susie came through from the kitchen area. "Happy Thanksgiving!"

Susie echoed Mack's words, proud of him despite their grievous loss. She came forward, smiled down at the baby, then hugged her old friend. The hug didn't seem forced, even after their recent hardship. It seemed sincere and good, Susie to the max. "Happy Thanksgiving,

Gabe. I'm so glad you're all right, and that Tee is okay." She winced in empathy. "That had to be such a scare for Corinne. I'm not sure I could handle that kind of thing. I'd have been turned inside out."

"I think she'd agree with that assessment one hundred percent," Gabe told her. He motioned to the living room. "Can we sit?"

"Yes, of course, you're probably tired." Susie moved forward. Gabe followed, set the baby seat on the couch and undid Jess's straps.

The beautiful, perfect baby gave him a happy, blue-eyed stare, as if pondering their earlier conversation, then grinned.

He grinned back, kissed her cheek and gently touched his forehead to hers, hoping and praying he could do this right. He took one deep, lingering sniff of Jessie's sweetness, then turned and set the nearly five-month-old baby into Susie's arms. "Here you go."

"Oh, Gabe." Susie's eyes went damp as she dropped her gaze, but not before he read the longing in her eyes. "She's growing."

"She is. And she eats a lot. And she still likes to wrestle me awake at night, so prepare yourselves to take the occasional nap."

Mack frowned. "Do you need us to baby-sit?"

"Here's what I need." Gabe set the car seat

onto the floor and sat down. "I need you to take her and be the best parents you can possibly be to her. I'm pretty sure you can do that, right?"

Susie swallowed hard, staring at him with wide eyes, instinctively holding the baby a little closer. A little tighter. "What?"

Mack leaned forward, concerned. "Gabe, you can't be serious. If this is because you think you can't do a good job with a kid, man, you're wrong. So wrong." He got up and paced away, then back. "You'll be a great dad to her." He nodded to Susie. "We both know that. You need to kick the self-doubt to the curb and believe in yourself again. You saved a kid's life yesterday, Gabe. That's got to be worth something, right?"

Gabe had watched Mack run his hand through his hair, pace the floor and then stop in front of him, face-to-face. He held Mack's gaze. "Are you done?"

Surprise furrowed Mack's brow. "Yes."

"Good. Listen." He turned to include Susie in his line of vision. "I love you guys. You've been with me through thick and thin, you stuck by me through the bad years and the worse years, and I know I can always count on you."

Susie reached out and touched a hand to his

leg. "That's what friends are for, Gabe. That's kind of like the meaning of the word, isn't it?"

Gabe knew it didn't always work out that way. Their special brand of friendship was a rare jewel. Seldom found and always treasured. "Yeah, but you know that runs amok for lots of folks. Anyway, Jessie needs a home. Her grandparents will do everything they can to undermine her happy existence within our family, and what way is that to start a beautiful new life?"

"There are jerks in every family, Gabe." Mack uttered the words, but Gabe heard the note of hope and wonder in his voice. "You can't be serious."

"I'm quite serious. You'll have to go through the proper channels with the county for adoption, and I'd like to be considered as her godfather when the need arises, but if you'd like to become parents sooner rather than later, I'll be glad to have the lawyer draw up the change of custody papers on Monday and we can get the process going."

"Sooner, meaning…?"

Gabe stood, leaned down and kissed Susie's cheek. They were tear-stained once more, but this time for a very different reason. "How does now sound?"

"You're serious." Mack stared at him, open-mouthed, while Susie rose with a now-fidgety baby.

"Come help me unload the portable crib."

"You packed it?"

"I figured if you said yes, you'd need it, and you can return it to Drew and Kimberly when you're done because I'm willing to bet the kid's going to get a really cute nursery makeover." He grinned at Susie.

"Gabe, are you sure? Really sure?" She gripped his arm, then hugged him, baby and all. "I don't even know how to talk you out of it, because I'd much rather just scream 'yes!' and be done."

"She doesn't like screaming, so just love her, okay? Love her like her young mother wanted her loved, in a way my cousin never knew in all of her twenty-one years. Just love her the way God loves his people."

"We will." Susie gripped his arm tighter as tears streamed down her cheeks. "Oh, we will do that so happily, my friend."

"Good. What are you guys doing for Thanksgiving?"

They exchanged guilty looks that Gabe had anticipated because celebrating Thanksgiving had probably been the last thing on their sorrowed minds.

"I thought as much. I'm going to see if the

Gallaghers have room for two more. I expect they do. I promised them we'd have Thanksgiving together, but I think it would be nicer to have all of Jessie's family there. Me. Her Auntie Corinne. And her new mom and dad."

"Dad." Mack ran his hand through his hair again, clapped his hands together, then paused. "I'm a dad."

Susie nodded.

Did she know she was crying? Did she care?

Gabe had no idea as he and his best friend unloaded a car full of baby things into Mack and Susie's living room.

They set up the crib and arranged the necessities, and when things were somewhat organized, Gabe squared his shoulders.

This was the hard part.

He'd done the easy part because he knew it was the right thing to do. He'd known it when the wind and ice and snow pelted his face and arms the day before. And when he'd gone to Kate Gallagher's to pick up the happy baby, he knew it would be his last time doing it, and not because he wasn't capable.

He'd learned his lesson about that.

He knew because this was the right thing to do after seeing his aunt and uncle last weekend. Jessie MacIntosh would start life with a new name and a clean slate, a gift bestowed on her by the mother and cousin who loved her enough to put her needs first.

"Bye, pumpkin."

His eyes grew moist as he bent to kiss her.

She reached up for him, to play with his face. His nose. His eyes.

And then that sweet baby made everything easier by smiling at him, then burrowing her tired little self into Susie's loving arms.

It would all be fine.

He'd been sure of it mentally, and now he was sure of it completely. "I'll see you guys later."

"Three o'clock?"

"That's what Kate said. Just in time to eat before the late-game kickoff."

"Gabe."

He turned.

Mack grabbed hold of Gabe's hand, then hugged him instead. "I love you, man. We both do."

"It's mutual. I'll see you in a few hours, for the best Thanksgiving I've had in a long time. Okay?"

"Okay."

He strode to the empty vehicle, refusing to dwell on what he'd just given up because he'd figured out yesterday that none of this was about him.

It was about others, just as it should be, and just like his mother taught him years ago.

He climbed into the car and didn't look at the suddenly empty space. Instead, he steered the car toward the lake because it was time for him and his neighbor to have a little talk. He wasn't sure what her side of the conversation would be, but he knew what he wanted to say... and then he'd take it from there.

His sound system advised him of an incoming call as he took the turn toward Canandaigua Lake. He recognized the name in the hands-free display and pulled onto the road's shoulder. He hadn't talked to Elise's sister in a long time. That made him fairly certain that whatever she had to say after all this time was better with his full concentration. "Amelia?"

"Gabe." He noted the hesitancy in her voice and waited.

"I saw the news report about you today," she continued. Now anxiety mixed into her tone. "How you rescued that girl, caught in the storm."

It was the kind of story the press ate up on a holiday, so the downstate coverage wasn't a big surprise to him. "I'm just glad it worked out the way it did. How are you, Amelia?" She'd taken the loss of her niece and sister hard, and she hadn't talked to him since a few months after Elise's funeral. And that discussion hadn't gone well for either of them.

"I'm okay, Gabe. I'm—" She drew a harsh breath then raced on. "I'm calling to apologize. I should have done this a long time ago, and I didn't and that makes me a horrible person, Gabe. And I'm sorry about that." Another short gasp indicated she was fighting tears and losing. "So sorry."

"Amelia, you're not a horrible person." Hadn't God been teaching him that same lesson lately? To unleash the shackles of the past and move on? To embrace the future God laid so lovingly before him?

"I am, Gabe," she went on in a stronger voice. "Because I'm the only one who knew what really happened that day, and I never told anyone because I promised my sister I wouldn't. I said nothing, not to my parents, my husband or my friends. It's been eating me alive for years, and when I saw that picture of you after that rescue yesterday, and that look in your eyes..." She stopped, and he heard her trying to catch her breath. "I realized you hadn't moved on like I hoped. That you still wore that guilt like a weight around your neck, and it wasn't fair. Not one bit fair."

"Amelia." He kept his voice soft but firm. "It's a long time ago. We've both got to go forward."

"But I can't. Not until I tell you the truth, Gabe. You didn't leave that car door open that day. Elise did."

Every hair on the back of his neck stood straight up. What did she say? That Elise had left their car door ajar the day they lost their beloved child?

An adrenaline buzz kicked in. He gazed out the window, seeing the upper curve of the lake in front of him. Yesterday's waves had calmed to a placid blue, lapping the sand along the north-end beach in a gentle give-and-take while his pulse roared like a wild ride in his ears. "What do you mean, Amelia?"

"She confessed to me, Gabe." Her voice went soft. "I told her she should come to you, that you'd understand, but she couldn't face the truth. She knew you'd be disappointed in her, and that you didn't like her drinking when she was with the other moms.

"She made me promise not to tell, and I thought once she was gone, that you'd move on with your life. I imagined you married, with kids, and everything nice and normal. I convinced myself that keeping my sister's secret preserved her memory for our family, but it's been eating at me like crazy lately. When I saw your face in that picture, I realized what losing Gracie did to you, and that I was the only one who could speak the truth and rid you of that horrible guilt. I'm just so sorry it took me this long. Forgive me. Please."

Elise left the door open.

He scrubbed his hands to his face, thinking. It all made sense. Her reaction, the drinking, the guilt and then her untimely death.

"I've felt guilty ever since she told me, because what if I'd come to you, Gabe? What if I'd had the courage to break my promise and tell you what happened? Could we have saved my sister?" Grief deepened her voice. "I'll never know because I said nothing. And I've regretted it ever since."

So much guilt. So many regrets. So much pain.

Forgive us our trespasses, as we forgive those who trespass against us...

Gabe swallowed hard.

A kaleidoscope of images danced through his brain. Elise. Grace. Corinne. Tee. Baby Jessie in Susie's arms...

He drew a deep breath. "Amelia." He pinched the bridge of his nose, then said, "I forgive you. And I'll ask you to do the same for me."

"But, Gabe—"

"Elise liked to drink too much when she got together with the girls. I knew that. She'd promised she wouldn't overdo it that day, and it was only at parties, but I should have been double-checking things myself. I had promised to be the designated driver so she could relax, when I should have made it more important to be the designated parent."

He paused, then sat straighter in his seat. "We've all made mistakes, Amelia. It's Thanksgiving. A day to give thanks for what we have. How about if you and I make a pact that from now on, on every holiday, we look forward, not back? I think it's time for us to do that, don't you?"

"You don't hate me?"

He didn't. He felt sorry for her, and for himself, that they'd both allowed Elise's drinking to be treated casually until it was too late. And then everything had snowballed from that moment. "Not at all. I wish she'd told me. Maybe then we could have gotten through it together." He breathed in. "I'm glad you called, Amelia. I hope you have a blessed holiday."

"You, too."

She disconnected the call.

He sat in his seat, watching the water ebb and flow against the cream-colored sand on the lakeshore.

The snow hadn't lasted on the sand. It rarely did because even oblique sun rays were enough to heat sand quickly, melting the snow.

This tiny view of the lake offered new hope, a fresh start. And Amelia's phone call augmented that new beginning.

And yet it didn't matter now. Not really. Not like it would have. There was plenty of guilt to go around in any tragedy. He'd witnessed that often in his years on the force.

The clean slate along the water's edge called to him. He put the car into gear and edged onto Lakeshore Drive. He knew what kind of new beginning he wanted and needed, and he only hoped the lady in question felt the same way. If not?

He lived next door, and he wasn't afraid to use proximity to his advantage. He wanted a wife, and he wanted a family, and he wanted it all with Corinne.

He didn't want to give up being a cop. It was who he was, and what he did.

But he had every intention of convincing her that loving a cop was worth the risk involved.

Chapter Seventeen

Corinne parked her car along the narrow stone path of the Grace Haven Cemetery like she always did. She and Tee climbed out one side of the car. Callan stepped out of the other. Together they crossed the shallow incline to the patriotic garden and simple monument marking David Gallagher's grave.

Callan moved forward. He set a thick-stemmed pumpkin against the marbled gray stone, then three little gourds alongside it, one for each of them.

Tee tucked a small American flag into a potted chrysanthemum and set it to the right of the pumpkin. Corinne bent low and added a spray of three red roses, their salute of love for a man gone too soon.

She stood back up, quiet. They didn't have to talk or pray out loud when they visited Dave's grave. Words weren't necessary. But then Callan pointed to the thin script along the stone's center. They'd tucked one of Dave's favorite sayings there, just below his name and above the scripture notation. "Today *is* someday."

Dave had lived those words. He always pushed to get things done, not to put tasks off to a random someday. He was a doer, a take-charge kind of personality with a great sense of humor, much like his adolescent daughter, two peas in a pod, as Kate liked to say.

Callan braced his arms around his middle in a firm stance. "I've made a decision, Mom."

She looked his way and read his intent.

"I'm still aiming for baseball, but only two percent of people who want to play in the majors get to play in the majors."

She nodded. She knew the stats.

"If that doesn't work out, I'm going blue. Like Dad and Grandpa and Uncle Drew."

His pronouncement should have surprised her. Callan was more like her, careful, assessing and cautious, but gazing at the rapidly growing young man, she realized that those qualities would serve him well, no matter what he chose to do in life. She pulled in a deep breath and smiled. "This isn't the shock you think it is."

"No?" He'd looked worried to make the announcement, but a little excited, too.

"It's in your blood, Callan. It's a bond that's never broken, even by death. A brotherhood of officers."

"You won't try to stop me because of what happened to Dad?"

She might have, a few months ago. She might have two days ago, before Gabe swooped in to rescue her daughter.

Now...she shook her head. "Your dad and I would both want you to follow your conscience, Cal. To do what you think God wants you to do. And if that is serving your community as an officer, I will be proud of your service. Every single minute of it."

He looked relieved by her words. He turned and offered a short salute to Dave's grave, but not to the lifeless stone or pretty autumn arrangement.

To his father, gone before the kids really had a chance to know him.

"Are we going back home before we go to Grandma's?" Tee asked.

"No, we've got everything we need in the car. Let's head that way. Aunt Kimberly is bringing a frozen pumpkin ice cream pie from Stan's custard stand, and I'm going to take a little of my own advice today and eat dessert first."

"Whoa." Tee flashed her a teasing grin. "Mom is walking on the wild side!"

"Totally," Callan added in a dry tone. "But if Mom gets to do it, we all get to do it, so what are we waiting for?"

"Race!" Tee was off like a flash. Callan, too. They hit the car at the same time, laughing like the delightful normal kids they were.

She didn't cry as she faced the grave. She read the inscription again, out loud. "Today *is* someday."

A day for new choices and new roads. Dave wouldn't have wanted her to live her life worried. He'd have teased her out of her funk and moved on, and that's what she needed to do now. She'd probably messed up her chance with Gabe Cutler. She'd read the angst on his face the previous day, and she hadn't even gotten a chance to properly thank him for rescuing Tee. He must think her ungrateful and stupidly stubborn.

She'd thank him today.

She'd make sure everyone knew how grateful she was for the rescue and for him. Just him.

She strode to the car, determined to make things right. She climbed in and turned the key.

Nothing.

She frowned, checked to make sure the steering wheel was locked and tried again.

Still nothing.

"It won't start?" Tee leaned up and over the seat.

"For real?" Callan asked. He pulled out his phone before she could say anything and hit a number. "Coach, we're stuck in the cemetery. Mom's car won't start and we're in danger of missing pumpkin ice cream pie. Can you save us? Again?"

Heat climbed Corinne's cheeks. Callan hit the speaker button, and Gabe's voice came through loud and clear. "On my way. Be there in ten minutes."

Drew and Kimberly pulled in ahead of them. They trekked to the grave, adorned it with a holiday wreath. They paused, gazing down, remembering Drew's best friend and Kimberly's big brother...and then they came their way. "Why are you sitting in the car in the cemetery?"

"Car won't start."

"No?" Drew arched his brows. "I'll call Grant."

"Coach is on his way to rescue us," Tee told them, hanging out her window. "I think this is getting to be a thing. We get into trouble—"

"Or cause trouble," Callan deadpanned with a look in Tee's direction.

"—and then Coach rescues us."

"Well, how about if we take you two with us? Because that ice cream pie is waiting at the house, and as much as I love the Gallagher clan, I don't trust them to leave the pie alone until after dinner."

Tee poked Corinne's shoulder. "They're on to us, Mom."

"So it would seem." She turned her gaze back to Drew and Kimberly. "You guys don't mind taking them?"

Drew opened Tee's door. "Of course not, although I feel funny leaving you here alone."

"I'm fine. And Gabe will be here soon."

"We could just call him and tell him we're rescued," Tee suggested. "Save him a trip."

"It's on his way, and there's food at Grandma's," noted Kimberly.

"Reason enough to ride with you guys." Callan fist-pumped the air as he loped to their car. "Tell Coach I'll save him a piece."

Corinne shot Kimberly a quick look of thanks. She wanted a minute or two alone with Gabe, long enough to apologize and thank him. Kimberly and Drew pulled out of the knoll about two minutes before Gabe pulled in.

He parked his SUV, climbed out and came her way.

Her heart sped up. She started to climb out of the car, but he leaned down, blocking the door. "What seems to be the problem, ma'am?"

She gazed into his gorgeous light brown eyes, sparked with humor and something else. Something deliciously indefinable. "My car won't start, Officer."

"That's 'Trooper,' ma'am."

She inclined her head with a slight smile as she corrected herself. "Trooper."

He grinned, held her gaze, then stepped back. "Pop the hood."

She did.

He gave a look underneath as she climbed out of the car. "Do you see anything?"

He shook his head. "No. But then I use Frank at Pieroni's Garage because I know nothing about engines. I called him on my way. He should be here soon."

"But you had me pop the hood." She moved toward him, puzzled.

"For effect." He straightened as she laughed, and then he looked around. He spotted the fresh arrangement of tributes on the incline and jutted his chin. "Your husband's grave?"

"We stop by on holidays or just any old day.

I've always wanted to give the kids a sense of who Dave was, because they never got a chance to know him personally. Callan was a toddler when he died, and I was pregnant with Tee."

"That's a tough set of circumstances."

It had been, so she acknowledged it with a lift of her shoulder. "But we did okay."

"You did more than okay. Corinne, listen—" he began, but she had started in at the same time.

"Gabe, I—"

They both paused. Gabe motioned her to go ahead. "Ladies first. Are you cold? Because we can talk in my car. It's got heat and everything. Unlike yours that won't turn on."

"I'm fine. And I've got to say this to you, and it's easier face-to-face."

He waited solemnly, but his eyes still twinkled, as if he had a secret. A happy kind of secret, and she liked seeing him that way.

"I want to thank you for yesterday." He waved that off as no big deal, but Corinne knew better. "Don't brush it off, Gabe Cutler. You risked your life and sacrificed your boat to save my daughter. I can't even begin to tell you how scared I was when that call came in, and then to be stuck in traffic, unable to get here quickly."

"Horrible, I expect."

She nodded, then shrugged. "It was and it wasn't. It was the wake-up call I needed." She drew a deep breath and looked up. "I've been so busy trying to be a great mom and trying to keep them safe and sound, proving I could do it all, that I lost track of some of the important things. I forgot to trust in God, because when I *did* trust him, I lost Dave. I think I never quite forgave God for that, and couldn't hand over the reins because I'd been let down before. And even though I know it was a human decision that put my husband in harm's way..." She hesitated. "He took a chance that day and lost. I still felt like God let me down."

"And now?"

"I realized as I drove home yesterday, completely powerless to help, that I've gotten power hungry," she admitted. "I like being the decision maker. I like being the person in charge. That power is being wrenched out of my hands as the kids grow up, and I realized yesterday that it was never really in my hands. I wanted it to be, but the true power and strength was beyond me. And with Him. He sent you to me. He sent you to coach my son, and He sent you this year to be my next-door neighbor." She put her hands on his arms. "And you saved my little girl's life. I can never thank you enough for that."

Chapter Eighteen

Gazing down into her pretty blue eyes, he could think of several ways, all of them amazing and wonderful, but he didn't have the right to make fear a central part of her life. "I love being a cop, Corinne."

She held his gaze and didn't blink.

"It became my stronghold when I lost my daughter, and then my wife. I couldn't help them, but I could make amends by helping others, and that meant so much to me."

"Did it mean enough to take foolish risks?"

He shook his head firmly. "It meant enough to do what needs to be done. My love for police work isn't about the perils. It's about keeping people safe. Helping others. And sometimes, catching the bad guys, because that's part of the job. But mostly, it's about watching out for danger and avoiding it before it happens. I love what I do, Corinne. I haven't always loved who I am, but I love what I do. And I need you to be okay with that. And to be okay with this." He pulled out his phone, swept open a picture and held it up. "I'm signing custody of Jessie over to Mack and Susie."

Her eyes went wide. She looked at him, the photo, then him again. "You're giving them the baby?"

"It's the right thing to do." He stared at the picture Mack and Susie had sent minutes ago, their first family selfie. And he smiled. "If I keep Jessie, my aunt will make sure my family stays fractured. To her, Jessie was born of sin and can't escape that, and I would never want Jessie to hear her hateful words of condemnation. This way I can ensure that never happens, and make two of the best people I know very happy."

"That's an incredible sacrifice." She whispered the words because she knew how much he'd bonded with Jessie, and how easy it would have been to keep her. "Gabe, you're amazing."

He wasn't, but it felt good to hear her say it.

"Truly amazing." She gripped his arms again, and the look she gave him, as if he were something special and wonderful and true... it was the kind of look he'd like to see the rest of his life. "And inspiring," she whispered, her eyes locked on his.

"Well, I have an ulterior motive. But it hinges on you, and I'm not sure I should bring it up right now."

"Of course you should," she argued. "I want to know everything about you, Gabe. If you're willing to give me a second chance at this whole romance thing, we need to start with a clean slate. Don't you think?"

Oh, he thought so all right. He locked his hands around her waist and gazed down. "Here's what I'm thinking." He dropped his mouth to hers and kissed her, long and slow. "I think we should keep doing things like this forever. I think we should let ourselves be in love and stay in love and take Tee fishing a lot."

She laughed against his cheek, and it felt good to feel the warmth of her laughter ruffle his cool skin.

"And I'd like to have a family with you, Corinne."

"Gabe—" She sounded surprised, and she had good reason to be, because her kids were almost grown.

"I know you've done this all before." He kissed her cheeks, her ear, her forehead, and then took her mouth again. And when he stopped kissing her, he drew her up against his chest, holding her close. So close. "But I'd love to have another chance to raise kids. With you. If you're willing."

Willing?

Corinne was pretty sure her heart had just been swept away by this rugged lawman. "You're wondering if I'd be willing to have your baby, Gabe? Our baby?"

"That would be the question. And it's not a deal breaker, Corinne." He leaned back to see her face, still holding her. "There's nothing I want in this life more than you, and a chance to be a good friend and dad to Tee and Callan. But if you're willing to increase our family, I'd be the happiest man in town."

She reached up and kissed him. She kissed him until he was convinced of her answer with no words needed, then added the words. Just to be sure. "I would love to have more kids. And I would be honored to be your wife, if you ever get around to asking me, that is."

"Corinne." He snugged her close, then turned her loose and took a knee. "Corinne, I think I've been falling in love with you for a long while, but I was too stubborn to let myself be happy and you were too stubborn to flirt with me. Except you couldn't exactly help it."

She laughed because every word of that was truth.

"And while I make a really good neighbor, I'd like the chance to be an even better husband. Will you marry me?"

"In a heartbeat."

He kissed her again.

Frank's tow truck rumbled into the far lane. He backed the rig up to Corinne's vehicle, hoisted it onto the bed, wished them a happy Thanksgiving and was back on his way in less than five minutes.

Corinne turned toward Gabe. "I'd like a Christmas Eve wedding."

His eyes went wide before he grinned. "Four weeks away. Perfect. We don't want to interrupt the winter baseball practice season with wedding planning."

She laughed and looped her hands around his neck. "Nope. That's not why I want to hurry. This is." She gave him a most convincing kiss. "We've already spent too much time apart. I'm totally unwilling to waste another minute of not being your wife, but with two wedding planners in the family, I'll be killed if I don't give them at least a few weeks to plan things."

* * *

Gabe couldn't possibly be happier than he was at this moment.

To spend Christmas with Corinne by his side. With Tee and Callan at church and at the Gallagher family dinner. And here, on the solemn grounds of Grace Haven Memorial Cemetery, commending their father. As it should be. "It sounds perfect. And now we should go because I think we just let Frank drive off with the apple pie and the cranberry relish."

"No!" She stared down the now-empty lane and sighed. "It was a really good pie, too."

"I bet it was, but we've already pulled him out once on the holiday. We could chase him down…" he supposed.

"Or we can call him and tell him to take it into town when he visits his dad in the hospice house."

Gabe thought he couldn't love her more.

He was wrong.

He texted Frank to take the pie and cranberry relish to share with others as Corinne climbed into the car. He climbed in beside her, turned the car on, then turned her way. "You ready for this, my love?"

She feathered a kiss to his cheek, a kiss of faith, hope, love and promise. "I am."

He put the car in gear and drove down the lane, then out onto the road.

A new chance.

A new beginning, for both of them, and for Jessie, too.

As he drove toward town, church bells chimed in unison, marking the hour in joyful abandon. And when they were done tolling, the old stone church carillon rang out the poignant notes of "How Great Thou Art" for the entire town to hear, a Grace Haven Thanksgiving tradition.

And it was good.

Chapter Nineteen

Gabe tucked extra twinkle lights, a fresh evergreens wreath and baby clothes into the back of the car, then spotted a missed call from Corinne. He called her back, delighted by his list of accomplishments.

She answered quickly. Too quickly for a pregnant woman who was supposed to spend the next three weeks resting. "You're supposed to be off your feet. I told you I'd handle everything, didn't I?"

"You did, and I'm beyond blessed, but darling, there's one thing you can't handle, and it's this. I'm in labor."

He couldn't have heard her correctly, because his son and daughter weren't due for nearly three weeks. "You can't be."

"Well, I tried telling the twins that, but they seem to have a mind of their own. Stubborn little things. Oh…" She started breathing in that way women do as a contraction takes hold and won't let go.

"Honey. Honey, I'm on my way, and I've got the twinkle lights!"

She laughed and spoke quickly. "Dad's bringing me and the kids to the hospital. Meet us there. And I think it would be best to leave the twinkle lights in the car."

He knew that. Could anyone blame a guy for being a tad nervous when his beautiful wife was carrying not one, but two tiny babies?

He stopped shopping for the perfect Christmas decorations she thought she needed to make things just right, climbed into the driver's seat and drove to the hospital in Rochester. Corinne's doctor didn't anticipate problems, but she wanted Corinne in a facility with an NICU in case the babies came early or needed extra help.

By the time he got up to the third floor, Corinne had been admitted and full-blown panic set in.

How could he do this? How could he put her through this? What if something happened to her? Or to the babies?

Pete intercepted him, smacked him on the back and met his look, man-to-man. "It will be fine. I promise."

Pete couldn't promise that. No one could. "You don't know that."

"Maybe not, but if you go into that room—" he pointed to the waiting room behind him where Kate and the kids had gathered "—or that one—" he pointed through the locking double doors separating them from the labor and delivery unit "—looking scared, I'll mop the floor with you."

His tough words helped. Plus, Gabe was pretty sure Pete meant it. He breathed deep, then stopped by the waiting room door. When Tee and Callan spotted him, he jerked a thumb toward the birthing center. "I'm going in, and I'll keep you guys updated, okay?"

"Yes." Callan nodded, calm but concerned.

Tee practically bounced in her seat. "I can't wait!"

A nurse appeared behind him. "Mr. Cutler? We're getting close, and your wife is refusing to deliver either baby until you're with her."

Close? That was impossible. Wasn't it? "She just got here. Are you sure?"

"Reasonably certain." She held the door for him, winked at the family and then showed him where to wash up and grab a gown.

He jumped into the hospital-issued clothing and rushed to Corinne's room.

"Gabe." She looked up at him as a contraction rocked her. He grasped her hand, wishing he could do more, wishing he could—

And then Jacob Gabriel appeared into the world, all six pounds, four ounces of him, and Gabe Cutler fell in love all over again. With his wife, with his life and with this amazing creation who squalled for short seconds, then paused, peeking here and there as if wondering what just happened.

"How is he?" Corinne pushed herself more upright to see, but Gabe brought the tiny fellow down to her level. "Is he fine? He's so quiet."

"He's perfect," the doctor declared. "Absolutely perfect, Corinne. And it's not going to take long to deliver his sister, so be ready. And it might have been a while for you, but remember—" the doctor smiled at her "—a quiet baby isn't necessarily a bad thing."

"Those are true words," she whispered, gazing on the wonder of her baby son. But then the rise of another contraction pulled her attention in another direction. "Hang on to him, Gabe." She laid her hand against baby Jacob's hospital blanket and whispered the words up to him. "I want him to know how much we love him even when I'm busy with his sister."

"I've got him, darling," he promised as the contraction took hold. "I won't let go. I won't let go of any of you."

"And here we go again." The doctor smiled at Corinne over her surgical mask. "You're doing great, Corinne."

Weighing in at nine ounces less than her brother, Isabella Katherine Cutler made her appearance, and let the entire room know she wasn't all that happy about the environmental changes she'd just endured.

Baby Jacob blinked twice, snuggled into Gabe's chest and dozed off, ignoring his sister's newborn theatrics.

"How we doing, Dad?" Corinne reached up a hand to him as the NICU crew checked Isabella.

How was he doing?

There were no words, but he tried. He slipped into the chair next to her bed, leaned in and kissed her sweetly. Gently. And then he laid his forehead to hers. "I have never been happier in my life. That's how I'm doing."

"Me, too."

They brought Isabella to Corinne, wrapped in a traditional hospital blanket. They'd snugged a tiny pink crocheted hat onto her head, and a blue one on Jacob. And then one of the nurses began to take a photo. "First family shot," she announced, happily.

Gabe stood, messing up the shot. He handed her the baby and said, "Hold that thought." He hurried down the hall, through the doors, and had Callan and Tee come back into the room with him. "Big brother and sister have to be in on the act," he explained. "It's not a family shot without them."

"That's right," Corinne agreed.

Eyes wide, the older kids took a spot on opposite sides of the hospital bed, and when the nurse snapped the picture, she held up the camera for all of them to see. "You are now a family of six."

"Perfect." Corinne smiled at the kids, then him, and the two utterly beautiful babies that had just joined the family. "Everything is absolutely perfect."

And it was.

* * * * *

If you loved this story,
pick up the other books
in the GRACE HAVEN *series*
from author Ruth Logan Herne:

AN UNEXPECTED GROOM
HER UNEXPECTED FAMILY
THEIR SURPRISE DADDY

Available now from Love Inspired!

Find more great reads at
www.LoveInspired.com

Dear Reader,

I love writing holiday stories. I go a little crazy with twinkle lights, ornaments, heartwarming nativities and Christmas movies! I love the music, the warmth of hymns and carols. I have so much fun decorating and baking and getting together with family. I love the church services, filled with light and hope. I love all of it.

But people who've suffered loss may have a very different experience with holidays. The grief, guilt and sorrow can weigh heavily during the holiday season. That was Gabe Cutler's life since losing his daughter and wife. He buried himself in work every November, and didn't emerge until the New Year. In his heart, he couldn't forgive himself for what happened that fateful day, years before.

Corinne blocked herself in a different way. Her loss made her a little control-crazy. She loves her children, but their growing independence rocks her world. She needs to adjust... and it takes a near-tragedy to show her the true lessons of life.

I'm always amazed by God's timing, and I'm always blessed by the warm responses I get from readers. I love hearing from you! Feel free to friend me on Facebook, come by my website to see what's happening in Ruthy's world right now, and join me in Seekerville (seekerville.blogspot.com) or the Yankee Belle Café (yankeebellecafe.blogspot.com), where I partner with other delightful authors to talk about faith, family, food…and (of course!) romance!

God bless you and wishing you the very best holiday season ever!

Ruthy

Get 2 Free Books,

Plus 2 Free Gifts—

just for trying the Reader Service!

Get 2 Free Books,
Plus 2 Free Gifts—
just for trying the Reader Service!

HARLEQUIN

HEARTWARMING™

HOMETOWN HEARTS ♥

YES! Please send me **The Hometown Hearts Collection** in Larger Print. This collection begins with 3 FREE books and 2 FREE gifts in the first shipment. Along with my 3 free books, I'll also get the next 4 books from the Hometown Hearts Collection, in LARGER PRINT, which I may either return and owe nothing, or keep for the low price of $4.99 U.S./ $5.89 CDN each plus $2.99 for shipping and handling per shipment*. If I decide to continue, about once a month for 8 months I will get 6 or 7 more books, but will only need to pay for 4. That means 2 or 3 books in every shipment will be FREE! If I decide to keep the entire collection, I'll have paid for only 32 books because 19 books are FREE! I understand that accepting the 3 free books and gifts places me under no obligation to buy anything. I can always return a shipment and cancel at any time. My free books and gifts are mine to keep no matter what I decide.

262 HCN 3432 462 HCN 3432

Name _____ (PLEASE PRINT)

Address _____ Apt. #

City _____ State/Prov. _____ Zip/Postal Code

Signature (if under 18, a parent or guardian must sign)

Mail to the **Reader Service**:
IN U.S.A.: P.O. Box 1867, Buffalo, NY. 14240-1867
IN CANADA: P.O. Box 609, Fort Erie, Ontario L2A 5X3

HHBPA17

READERSERVICE.COM

Manage your account online!

- Review your order history
- Manage your payments
- Update your address

> **We've designed the
> Reader Service website
> just for you.**

Enjoy all the features!

- Discover new series available to you, and read excerpts from any series.
- Respond to mailings and special monthly offers.
- Browse the Bonus Bucks catalog and online-only exculsives.
- Share your feedback.

Visit us at:
ReaderService.com